FLAMES OF THE TIGER

FLAMES OF THE TIGER

John Wilson

Kids Can Press

Kids Can Press acknowledges the financial support of the Ontario Arts Council, the Canada Council for the Arts and the Government of Canada, through the BPIDP, for our publishing activity.

Published in Canada by
Kids Can Press Ltd.
29 Birch Avenue
Toronto, ON M4V 1E2

Published in the U.S. by
Kids Can Press Ltd.
2250 Military Road
Tonawanda, NY 14150

www.kidscanpress.com

Edited by Charis Wahl
Designed by Carolyn Sebestyen
Cover designed by Karen Powers
Cover image of boy courtesy of CORBIS/MAGMA
Cover image of tiger-tank replica courtesy of Pat Dillon Antiques, Toronto

Roads to Moscow: Words and Music by Alistair Ian Stewart. © Copyright 1973 Polygram Division Default on behalf of Gwyneth Music Ltd. International Copyright Secured. All Rights Reserved

Printed and bound in Canada

CM 03 0 9 8 7 6 5 4 3 2 1
CM PA 03 0 9 8 7 6 5 4 3 2

National Library of Canada Cataloguing in Publication Data

Wilson, John (John Alexander), 1951–
        Flames of the tiger / John Wilson.

ISBN 1-55337-618-8 (bound).   ISBN 1-55337-619-6 (pbk.)

I. Title.

PS8595.I5834F58 2003   jC813'.54   C2002-906158-X
PZ7

Kids Can Press is a *CORUS*™ Entertainment company

For all the victims of the Nazis:
those who were damaged in spirit
as well as in body

Two broken Tigers on fire in the night
Flicker their souls to the wind
I wait in the line for the final approach to begin …
The flames of the Tigers are lighting the road to Berlin.

Al Stewart
"Roads to Moscow"

Dieter peered over the lip of the ditch. The acrid smell of burning diesel fuel irritated his nose. Across the field, a burning Tiger tank lay stark and black against the sunset's fragile colors, its long cannon pointing uselessly at the heavens. Deep red flames licked upward from pools of spilled fuel, and a column of heavy, roiling smoke rose in the still evening air. A dead man lay on the scorched grass nearby, and another, his charred body arched in a final agony, was trapped half out of the tank's open hatch. Slowly Dieter scanned the field for signs of life — there were none.

He let out a long breath and relaxed.

"Is it all right?" an urgent whisper came from behind him.

The boy slithered back down the slope until he was lying beside his sister. "I think so. There's a tank in the field, but everyone's dead."

Dieter looked up at the sky. The pink of the setting sun on the thunderheads competed with the reflected glow of the burning village the pair had passed through that afternoon.

"This is as good a place as any to spend the night," Dieter said. "If the clouds bring rain, we'll cross to those trees or shelter under the tank if it's stopped burning by then."

Dieter extracted his water bottle and took a sip. His mouth was dry, and the desire to gulp the bottle empty was powerful, but he forced himself to stop and pass it to Greta.

"Just a sip," he warned.

"I know, I know," Greta replied. "Stop nagging." She took a sip and passed the bottle back. Dieter screwed on the top and replaced it in his pack. He pulled out a loaf of stale black bread, the last of the food Uncle Walter had given them two days before. It was coarse and unpleasant, but better than the sawdust-filled stuff they'd had in Berlin. In the long run, the bread would make Dieter's thirst worse, but he promised himself another sip of water when it was finished. He broke the loaf in half and handed a piece to Greta.

She groaned. "I'd give anything for a cream pastry, loaded with jam," she said wistfully.

"Don't torture yourself," Dieter advised as he sullenly chewed. "This is all we've got. Besides, you never liked cream pastries."

"I did so," Greta responded indignantly.

One of his sister's most irritating habits was an ability to rewrite the past to suit her mood. Dieter had long ago learned that he couldn't win an argument when Greta had convinced herself of something, so he let it go and ate in silence.

Despite his own advice, Dieter couldn't stop his mind drifting back to better days. It was something he often did. His father had called it daydreaming and said it was a waste of time, but many times recently, Dieter's memories had helped him get through the present. A good day-dream was a treasure. Dieter's surroundings faded, time slowed, and the past opened up in his mind like a movie. Sometimes when it was happening, he felt as if he were two people — the one who could sit at his school desk or walk or even carry on a simple conversation, and the one who was reliving some wonderful event.

Right now, while the surface Dieter chewed a mouthful of stale bread by the glow of a burning tank, the real Dieter was thirteen years old and sitting at the formal dining room table in the family apartment on the Charlottenburger. It was three years ago, Christmas Eve dinner 1941. The German armies were sweeping victoriously over the Russian Steppes and everyone thought the war was as good as won. Elsa still cooked and cleaned for the family, and the curtains over the long windows didn't need to be closed against the bombers. Dieter could stand at the windows and look out over the Tiergarten to the distant buildings of the zoo. He loved the zoo, the view out the window and the ornate high-ceilinged rooms of the apartment, but his favorite thing in the whole world was the dining room table.

The shine on the table was deep and magical, a pond with cool liquid depths that Dieter's imagination could reach into to pull out all manner of strange life. But it *was* solid — solid enough to support the gleaming silverware and carved crystal glasses. And the tureens and servers and plates, piled high with steaming potatoes, vegetables and meat.

Glorious smells filled the room — the warm, rich odor of ham and turkey, the sharp, slightly sour smell of cabbage. And wonderful tastes were there for the sampling — the sweetness of his mother's famous strudels, the saltiness of the soup, the fresh crispness of a Waldorf salad.

Dieter's father, Ernst, sat at the head of the table, looking every inch the family patriarch with his old-fashioned bushy mustache. At the foot sat Dieter's mother, Eva, resplendent in lace. To one side were Dieter and his little sister, Greta. On the table beside her, glinting in the candlelight, lay her most precious possession, her flute. She had got it the previous March for her eighth birthday, and it went everywhere with her. All year, she had practiced with a devotion that bordered on fanaticism, and even Dieter had to admit that she was getting quite good. Ernst allowed the flute to be brought to the table on condition that Greta play them a tune after the meal.

Opposite Greta was Dieter's twenty-year-old brother, Reinhard, looking splendid in his immaculate new SS uniform. Reinhard took after their mother. With his blond hair, high cheekbones, sharp nose and firm chin, he was the ideal Aryan man. Dieter wished he was tall and fair like Reinhard, but he had inherited his father's softer features, round face, brown hair and short stature.

Reinhard and Ernst were discussing the government.

"But you must admit, Father," Reinhard said, "Hitler has done such a lot for Germany. The punishing provisions that the British, French and Americans forced on us in the Versailles Treaty after the Great War were crushing our country. Hitler stood up to them and they backed down. Our economy is secure, there is work for everyone, and we see no more of the street violence that the Communists caused a decade ago. The displaced German communities in Austria, Czechoslovakia and Poland have been brought back into a nation that is being steadily purified of the undesirable elements that have been holding us back for so long. The war is almost won. It is a new age. How can you not see that it is better than the old world you grew up in?"

"I agree that the Nazis have achieved a lot. Versailles was iniquitous, our economy was a dreadful mess, and I have no more love than you for Jews and Communists, but do not dismiss the values of my world so glibly. I know that my family was privileged. We had estates in East Prussia, servants and aristocratic friends in very high places."

"And dogs and ponies," Greta interrupted excitedly. "That's what I would have loved. Can we get a dog?"

Ernst laughed. "We live in an apartment, and you probably want a wolfhound."

"Oh yes. One of those big hairy ones with the long noses."

"It wouldn't be fair on the dog, Greta. Those animals need a lot of exercise. More than the occasional walk in the Tiergarten.

"And I accept a lot of what you say, Reinhard. Much of my world is gone, lost in the inflation of the twenties and the stock market crash of nineteen twenty-nine, but it was doomed long before that. The trenches of the Kaiser's war destroyed my world, but there were some worthwhile things left. We had standards: we believed it was important to behave in a certain way, to show respect to others and to comport ourselves in a civilized, sophisticated manner. This is what separated us from the rabble. And you forget that ten years ago, it was not just the Communists who rioted in the streets. The people who now sit in our government, and whom you admire so much, began by smashing people's heads in street battles. They are vulgar, crude and lower-class. To have them in charge is a reversal of the structure of any civilized society.

"When Hitler won the election in 1932, I was convinced that the Nazi government wouldn't last six months. I was wrong there, and I have to admit that they have done our country some good, but I cannot believe that such a bunch of boorish rabble-rousers can be good in the long term."

"Oh, Father," Reinhard said, "you are so old-fashioned. You have to change with the times. Germany is great again, and it wasn't class and elegant manners that got us here, it was action.

"If you want to see the real lower classes, look at the Russians. The Panzers and the Luftwaffe are unbeatable in the east — every battle produces hordes of Russian prisoners. These Slavs are hopeless. One good German soldier is worth a whole platoon of them. If it wasn't for the Jewish Communist political officers warping their simple minds and pointing machine guns at their backs to force them to attack, the war would be over by now. Moscow would have fallen and we would be marching through Red Square taking the *lebensraum*, the living space our destiny demands. Soon, solid Aryan stock would populate Russia."

Ernst sat silent for a long moment. Dieter sensed a change in the room. He fiddled nervously with his fork. At length, Ernst went on, but his voice was slower and his tone more serious. "And what would you do with the people already there?"

"Well," Reinhard sat back and launched into his favorite topic. "They will be resettled —

after we get rid of all the Jews and Communists, of course."

"What do you mean by 'get rid of'?" Dieter's father's voice was quiet, but his words cut through Reinhard's enthusiastic tirade. Dieter felt the tension mount. Where was this conversation going? Ernst and Reinhard stared at each other. Then Reinhard smiled. "There's no need to worry about them," he said. "They can work — for the greater good."

"As slave labor?"

Reinhard shrugged.

"Slave labor and then what?" Ernst persisted.

"Then nothing. They won't be allowed to reproduce, so they will simply die out."

"Simply die out!" Ernst's voice rose in anger. "Good God, man, even Slavs and Jews are human. What you are suggesting is barbaric."

Everyone else at the table sat in silence. Even Greta had nothing to say as her gaze moved nervously between her father and her brother. Only Reinhard seemed composed and comfortable. His smile didn't falter.

"You are wrong there, Father," he said. "*They* are the barbarians. History proves that it is we, the true Aryan stock, who are destined to rule. We would do so already if our genes had not been contaminated by inferior blood and if the

Jewish Conspiracy was not so powerful. My generation's task is to purify the German nation. To get rid of the contaminants, to return the Aryan stock to the purity that made it great in the past. Imagine it — a single race from the Asian steppes to the Atlantic coast! What a great day that will be. It is a difficult task requiring fortitude and persistence, but it must be done. The future demands it."

"Please," Eva pleaded. "It's Christmas."

"I'm sorry, but I cannot let this go." Ernst's voice was barely above a whisper. He addressed his apology to his wife, but he never took his eyes off his son.

"Reinhard," Ernst continued. "The future *demands* nothing. Do not use historical necessity as an excuse. The things we see around us and think so important are mere flotsam swept along by the river of time. We can no more shape the future to fit our petty desires than we can stop time. If it were possible to create the future, do you think the world would have gone through the madness and horror I saw in the Kaiser's war?

"In my war, I saw lines of men fall before our machine guns like long grass in the wind. It was a futile, horrible waste, but at least the men were soldiers, doing what soldiers have always had to do and paying the price soldiers have always paid. You are talking about controlling the lives of millions of civilians. We may not like them, or want them to live beside us, but they are human beings, and no one, however much semi-mystical nonsense they invent to support their views, is entitled to turn an entire people into slaves."

Dieter's fork clattered onto his plate with a noise that made Greta jump. Ernst ignored the interruption.

"You asked me earlier, Reinhard, if I could not see that your world is much better than mine. I see good things in it, but there is neither class nor compassion underlying it. Therefore, there are no checks against going too far. My generation made mistakes — some horrible ones, I admit that — but when I hear you talk of such things, I truly fear where these men you admire so much will lead us.

"You are my son. I have watched you grow from a baby, and I love you. But your mind has become twisted by self-centered demagogues spouting rubbish passed off as thought. You are an adult and must make your own decisions, for better or worse, but I will not have such claptrap at my dinner table."

Reinhard's smile had vanished as his father spoke, replaced by a look of grim determination.

Now he rose, pushing his heavy chair back with a long grating sound. Dieter could see the muscles in his jaw clenched in anger. "You are a fool, Ernst Hammer," Reinhard said. "The future is mine. You may rail against it, but it will swallow you as easily as it will the Slav hordes. You may not care if the family is dragged down with you, but I do. I shall do as you ask and bite my tongue in your little kingdom for their sakes. But remember that the large world outside is mine."

Reinhard strode toward the dining room door. With his hand on the latch, he turned and looked straight at Dieter.

"Dieter," he said, "be careful not to get stuck in this old man's past. The future is yours, too, and you must embrace your place in it or be crushed."

As Reinhard's footsteps echoed down the hallway, Dieter was a turmoil of emotions — he was being asked to choose between the two people he admired most in the world: the big brother who had taught him to play football and taken him fishing in the city's many canals and rivers, and the father who had taught him to both show and expect respect and told him stories of the different world he had grown up in.

Dieter felt he was being torn apart. He yearned for the simple, colorful past his father talked of, but he couldn't deny the seductive attraction of the dynamic world being created around him by people like his brother.

Slowly Dieter realized that everyone was looking at him. They seemed to be demanding a decision. Why did he have to be drawn into this? Why wouldn't everyone just leave him alone?

Tears pooled in the corners of Dieter's eyes. To hide them, he violently pushed back his chair and fled to his room, where he lay weeping on his bed.

Dieter felt tears trickle down his cheek. He was glad of the darkness, so Greta couldn't see him cry. He had to be strong and fulfill his promise to his father — and to do that, he needed to get some sleep.

Dieter looked over at his sister curled up on the ground, her flute tucked into the waistband of her dress. Soft snoring came from her small form. Dieter was continually amazed at Greta's ability to instantly fall asleep anywhere. It was a valuable gift, especially now. For days the pair had been hiking through the war-torn countryside of north Germany, sleeping rough and surviving on an occasional piece of bread and ditch water. Dieter doubted either of them could go much farther.

Huddling into a ball beside his sister, with his pack as a pillow, Dieter closed his eyes. He was cold and hungry, but too tired for that to matter. His last thought before he sank into sleep was that tomorrow, May 2, 1945, would be his seventeenth birthday.

+ + +

Stuttering machine-gun fire brought Dieter immediately awake.

"What's that?" Greta asked groggily.

"Sssh!" Dieter hissed. He crawled up the slope and peered across the field. The burning Tiger cast an eerie red glow over the desolate scene. The machine-gun fire was coming from the tank, and occasional white arcs of tracer bullets shot through the air. Dieter relaxed.

Sliding back down the slope, he reassured Greta. "It's just the ammunition in the tank going off."

Dieter dug his water bottle out of his pack and treated them both to a sip. He had no idea what time it was. It was dark and beginning to rain. Large drops thudded onto the dry ground. Dieter was tired, but the shock of his awakening and the cold rain meant it would be a long time before he could get back to sleep. He shivered.

As if in answer, Greta said, "I'm cold."

She wore only a light dress that was filthy and torn. Dieter at least had a suit. It was several sizes too big, but it was warm enough. He draped his jacket around Greta's shoulders.

"Thanks," she mumbled.

The generous gesture left Dieter with only a sweater, thin, old and full of holes. It did little to keep out the damp chill. Should they start traveling? That might be warmer than sitting still, and it would get them away from anyone attracted by the gunfire. Traveling at night was also usually safer. Even a few hours walking before dawn would put them that much closer to their goal.

"Come on," he said. "We might as well get going." Greta let out an annoyed grunt, but she stood.

Dieter shouldered his pack and led the way along the ditch at the edge of the field. It headed roughly west, approximately the direction they wanted to go, and it afforded them protection from the bullets flying around the field.

The ground was slippery and Dieter had to stop frequently to feel his way around obstacles. In about half an hour, they had almost reached the far side of the field.

It was then that Dieter fell over the body.

At first he thought it was just an irregularity in the ground, but as he pushed his hand out to help raise himself, he encountered the still-wet mass that had been the man's chest. In the horror of realization, Dieter flung himself to one side, knocking Greta down, and frantically wiped off the gore on the grass.

"Watch what you're doing," Greta said petulantly.

"Hey! Is that you?"

The strange voice coming from the darkness was close. It was speaking English.

"Tom," the voice continued plaintively, "can you hear me? We got that tank pretty good, huh? Biggest I've ever seen. And to hear it coming! That rumbling roar from the ground — sounded like the devil himself coming to get us. But we got it instead, didn't we, Tom? Boy, to see it brew up when the bazooka rocket hit it. That was something, all right ... but you can't hear me, can you, Tom? That damned tank blew a hole in you so big you could near see through it."

Dieter was barely breathing. He didn't understand much of what the man was saying, but he grasped enough to tell that he was rambling.

"And it's done for me, too, I figure. I want to sleep, Tom, but I won't wake up, will I? It's not fair, this close to the end. We've got them beat okay, and then you go and get your chest blown in and I go and get a bullet in the head. I'm so tired."

Dieter's mind raced. This must be the anti-tank crew that had destroyed the Tiger. But why hadn't their mates come to help? Could there be other soldiers close by? Dieter could just make out a darker shape in the shadows and adjusted his position to get a better look. The buckle on his pack rattled against a stone. The harsh noise set the wounded man off again. But this time he was speaking German.

"It's odd, Father," he said. "I lived in one Berlin and it looks like I'm going to die on the way to another. I'll miss you and Mom."

Hearing the man speak his own language gave Dieter courage. Keeping his eyes fixed on the dark shape, he risked a reply.

"My name is Dieter," he said. "Are you badly wounded?"

For a long moment there was silence.

"Dieter?" the soldier replied at last. "You want to change that. No good having a German name, that's what Father says. He called me Joe — good Canadian name, Joe — and changed our family name to Gordon. Used to be Gordeler, you know. Too German — changed it in the First War, 'fore

I was born. Everyone was doing it. Even changed the name of our town. Used to be Berlin. Now it's Kitchener. Father said it was a good thing, too. We should have Canadian names and live in a Canadian town."

The mention of Canada galvanized Dieter. Without considering the risk, he sat up.

"Canada!" he exclaimed. "You're from Canada?"

"'Course I am," Joe replied. "Me and Tom are the best damned bazooka men in the whole First Army. Least we were until ..." Joe's voice trailed off in sadness.

Dieter had to keep him talking. "Where are the other Canadians?"

"Not here, that's for sure. It's all Brits and Yanks. Only a few of us Canucks. Got seconded to Montgomery's army to destroy some tanks that were holding them up.

"Wow! That Tiger was big, eh, Tom? But we got him good."

Joe had lapsed back into English. Dieter's mind was racing. He had suspected he was close to the Allied positions — maybe this Joe could capture him.

Talking soothingly and with Greta following close behind, Dieter edged toward Joe's voice. "I want to go to Canada," he said. "My father was

captured by Canadians in the Great War, and he
said what good people they were. He wanted to
take the family to Canada after the war, but
Mother wanted to stay in Berlin. She always said
things would never be as bad as Father feared.

"She was wrong. But she is dead now. So is
Father, and probably Reinhard, too. Greta and I
are all that's left. Father told us that we should
try to go to Canada, that it was a good place.
Will you help us get to Canada?"

Dieter had reached the dark shape now. It was
propped up on a backpack and the remains of a
bazooka rocket launcher. The body was silent.
Dieter was afraid the man had died. He kept
talking, trying to get a response.

"You lived in a town called Berlin?" he asked.
"I lived in Berlin, but there is not much left of it
now. The bombers came every night, and what
they missed, the Russian guns destroyed.

"Why do you speak German? Father told me
they spoke French in Canada."

"Buttons!" Joe said abruptly.

"What?"

"Mr. Roschman's button factory. Beautiful buttons, made from some kind of African nut. Last
forever. But buttons're all plastic now and the
machines can't make plastic buttons. No call for
real buttons anymore. Poor Mr. Roschman.

"Father worked for him from the time he went over from Germany in nineteen-hundred. He was only fourteen. He's much older now. Do you know Mr. Roschman?"

"No," Dieter replied, "I don't."

"Mother made us speak German at home. Father said there was no point. He said that we were Canadian now, but Mother insisted."

Dieter moved closer. If only he could see what was wrong with the soldier. Then he remembered the flashlight in his pack. Perhaps there was some life left in the battery. Dieter dug around for the oval shape. It fitted perfectly into the palm of his hand. He pushed the switch up, and a narrow beam of weak light shone. Dieter pointed it at the soldier. He looked dead. His eyes were closed and his face, neck and shoulders were caked in dried blood. A long gouge, surrounded by matted hair, ran from the man's forehead to behind his ear. Dieter could see the white gleam of bone in the cut. He reached over and touched the man's shoulder. His eyes flickered open.

"You can't sleep," Dieter said. "You will die if you sleep."

"So tired," Joe slurred.

"Here, I will give you a drink." Dieter withdrew his precious water bottle, unscrewed the cap and poured a few drops into the wounded man's mouth. Suddenly Joe's hand shot out and grabbed Dieter's wrist. Forcing the bottle up, Joe drank greedily.

"No!" Dieter shouted. "You must not drink too much." With an effort, he pulled away the nearly empty bottle. The wounded man flopped back. His eyes were open now, but not fixing on any one thing.

"Joe!" Dieter implored. "Don't go to sleep."

The wound looked bad, and Dieter had no bandages. He couldn't let the man die. He had found a Canadian, just as he had promised his father he would. Now he had to keep Joe alive. Without any medicine, the only thing he could do was keep him from going to sleep. But how? Dieter had to keep talking. What about? Then Dieter had an idea. He would tell Joe about his life. It might not interest the young Canadian, but perhaps the sound of Dieter's voice would be enough to keep Joe awake until help arrived.

"I was born in Berlin," Dieter began, "in nineteen twenty-eight. Reinhard was already six years old, and Greta here wouldn't be born for another five years. Our family used to be wealthy, so Father said. He had been born in a big house on an estate with servants and horses, but by the time

I was born, most of the money was gone. Bad business deals and the Kaiser's war, I think. And the year after I was born, the stock market crashed. We weren't like the unemployed who slept in the parks, but my parents — mostly my mother — yearned after the old life."

"And me, too," Greta interrupted. "It must have been wonderful — I could have had a horse and a dog."

"Yes," Dieter agreed. "But we still had a good life. We lived in a big apartment overlooking the Tiergarten. We had a cook, and a woman came in to clean once a week. I loved the apartment ceilings. They had wonderful ornate moldings around the edges and in the center where the lights hung — masses of coiling vines loaded with fruit and flowers. I used to lie in bed or on the floor and imagine that the moldings were a forest filled with exotic animals and birds."

Dieter suddenly became self-conscious at his childish memories and glanced at Joe. The soldier had turned toward him, the dried blood on his forehead cracked as his brow furrowed in concentration. Joe's eyes still wandered, but they kept returning to Dieter's face. As he talked, Dieter's mind drifted until he could see and smell and taste his memories.

"The first thing I remember," Dieter said as his mind's eye filled with the image, "was a street full of bright red flags. I thought they were covered in blood."

Dieter was almost four, and Reinhard was taking him to see a parade. Ernst had not been keen — there had been trouble at earlier National Socialist rallies — but Reinhard had turned on all his blond, ten-year-old charm and won the day. Dieter was ecstatic. As the pair walked through the crowded streets, Dieter found his hand engulfed in his big brother's. Happily he gave the hand a squeeze. It was returned.

"Almost there," Reinhard said. "The parade should be on the next street."

Sure enough, the crowd was thickening and the noise increasing. It was becoming a little scary — Dieter was jostled by people who loomed far above him — and all he could see were legs. Dieter began to hang back.

"It's getting crowded, huh?" Reinhard said. Then, grasping Dieter beneath the arms, he swung him up and plopped him neatly on his shoulders. Dieter felt like he owned the whole world. He could see everything — ranks of men in uniform, brown and black, with glittering medals and badges in silver and gold. And a band! Playing such rousing marching songs. Dieter couldn't stop his small body bouncing to the beat of the drums and trumpets.

Reinhard laughed. "You like the music?" He began jumping from foot to foot in time. Dieter giggled wildly. It was all wonderful, but the thing he would lie awake that night remembering were the flags. Everyone in the crowd seemed to be waving one, and the flags the marching men carried were huge. It was as if they were marching under a forest of banners. Long red ones. Bright red — vivid against the brown and black of the uniforms and the onlookers' drab clothes. Each flag had a spotless white circle in the middle and, in its center, a stark, black, odd-looking cross. Dieter couldn't stop giggling. He was so happy.

"Here you are, son." A man standing beside Reinhard handed Dieter a small flag. "Wave it proudly. It's going to be Germany's flag one day. Then the world won't push us around anymore."

Dieter waved for all he was worth. It was the best day of his life.

On the way home, Dieter clutched his new flag. He looked up at his brother. "Reinhard, I want to be a soldier when I'm big."

Reinhard laughed. "Those men are not soldiers. The National Socialists wear uniforms so they are easy to recognize. Not like the Communists, who hide behind working clothes. You'll need to grow some before you can march in a parade. But the National Socialists have a youth program," he went on excitedly. "The Hitler Youth, named for the party leader. I'm going to join. You get a uniform and everything."

Dieter listened in awe. Reinhard was going to get a uniform!

When they got home, Dieter rushed along the corridor and leaped at his father. Laughing, Ernst picked him up and swung him around. "So," he said, "my boys had a good time."

"Yes, yes, yes!" Dieter exclaimed happily. "Reinhard's going to be a Hitler soldier."

Ernst stopped spinning and placed his son on the carpet. Reinhard stood a few steps back along the wide hallway. "He means the Hitler Youth, Father," he said. "They have meetings and sports events —"

"And they wear a uniform!" Dieter shouted.

Ernst ruffled Dieter's hair and looked thoughtfully at his older boy. "I don't recall you asking permission."

"I was going to," Reinhard said defensively. "I haven't joined yet. I only mentioned to Dieter that I might, that's all."

Ernst nodded slowly. "Those National Socialists are a rabble of troublemakers. I don't want our family associated with that sort."

"It's just a youth group," Reinhard said plaintively. "Alfred from school is going to join, too. They have camping trips and hikes in the forest — and we learn to build a fire and find our way with a compass."

Reinhard's face glowed with enthusiasm at all the wonderful things he would learn.

"I don't think it would do any harm." Their mother stood at the kitchen door, behind Ernst. "It's a youth group, like the Boy Scouts. It's not political. Besides, it would do Reinhard good to get out in the fresh air with boys his own age. Boys need to burn off their energy."

Ernst found himself smiling despite himself. "All right. All right, Eva my dear," he said, surrendering to the two-pronged attack. "One thing this old soldier knows is when to conduct a strategic withdrawal. Later I will think about

Reinhard's request. But right now, it is time to get you two grubby children cleaned up for dinner."

+ + +

Eight months after the parade, Dieter was crouched in front of the fire in the parlor. It was January, and the warmth from the flames was comforting after the raw cold of the streets. The pattern in the carpet had become a jungle of huge trees, deadly swamps and twining creepers, in which Dieter's lead cavalry soldiers, in their bright blue uniforms and gleaming helmets, battled valiantly against wild animals. The soldiers had been a Christmas gift, twelve of them nestling in a velvet-lined box. He had bought the animals at the zoo, just two days earlier. Dieter was always nagging his parents to take him to the zoo. He loved the monkeys, elephants and bears, but most of all he loved the old Bengal tiger, called Rajah, that lived in a large enclosure. Dieter always had to force himself to look at all the other animals on the way to Rajah, for once in front of the tiger, he would stand for ages. He was impressed by Rajah's coloring, his size and his frightening teeth when he yawned, but he adored Rajah's attitude. When the great beast stared coldly at passersby, he seemed to rule the whole zoo. Dieter was convinced that, if he wished, Rajah could smash out of his cage and rush through the streets, tearing apart whomever he pleased. The thought added an extra thrill to standing close enough to look into the great creature's yellow eyes.

Now Dieter had his own Rajah. Not as fearsome as the real thing, but frightening enough to terrify his shiny soldiers. All afternoon, the soldiers had battled the zoo animals. They had done well against the bears, buffalo and lions, but as soon as they appeared to be getting the upper hand, Rajah would leap into the fray — and he always won.

Dieter played on the floor between his parents. Eva, vastly pregnant with his sister-to-be, was knitting. Ernst sat in the big winged armchair, reading the newspaper with a worried look on his face. Elsa, the maid, housekeeper, cook and last of the servants that had attended Ernst's family on their Prussian estates, hummed quietly in the kitchen as she prepared dinner.

Reinhard wasn't home yet from his youth group meeting. Ernst had finally allowed Reinhard to join the Deutsche Jungvolk, the Hitler Youth for ten- to fourteen-year-olds. He was not allowed to wear his uniform in the house, but he had put it on in secret to show Dieter. Reinhard also told Dieter stories.

Dieter's favorite story was about a boy called Herbert Norkus. Although only a little older than Reinhard, Herbert had taken part in National Socialist street demonstrations. About a year ago, he'd been attacked and stabbed by Communists. Bleeding badly, Herbert knocked on a door seeking help, but the door was slammed in his face. Stabbed again, Herbert had struggled down the sidewalk, leaving bloody handprints on the walls. Reinhard said Herbert was a hero, but icy shivers went down Dieter's spine when he thought of the boy dying in the street.

With a thunderous crash, the front door of the apartment opened and Reinhard flew in, still in his uniform of brown shirt and black shorts.

Ernst put his paper down with a snap. "What is the meaning of this? You know you must change —"

"But Father," Reinhard interrupted, skidding to a halt. "Have you not heard the wonderful news? Hitler is Chancellor of Germany. There are to be torchlight rallies in the streets. It is a great day."

"I have heard the news," Ernst said calmly. "I do not agree that it is so wonderful, but great day or not, you will change your clothes before coming into this house."

"You don't understand!" Reinhard stood rigidly, fists clenched by his side. Dieter thought he looked wonderful — so tall and fair in his perfectly pressed uniform with its black crosses on the arms — and so determined.

Ernst stared silently at his older son. Reinhard dropped his defiant gaze. "Yes, Father," he said. Then, looking up again, "But can we at least watch the parade from the balcony?"

"Yes," Ernst said, "that would be acceptable. When you are changed and we have had supper, you may watch some of the parade before bed."

"Thank you," Reinhard said, hurrying out of the room.

"Are you being too hard on him?" Eva asked, looking up from her knitting.

"No," Ernst replied. "I fear we have not been hard enough. I let him join that organization because I thought it was harmless and the party would not be around for long. Now that swaggering Austrian corporal is Chancellor and his thugs sit in the Reichstag while supposedly intelligent people fawn over him. I fear for what this country is coming to."

"But this Hitler won't last. You said it yourself."

"Yes, I did," Ernst said slowly, "but now I am not so sure. I thought he would go the way of all the other pretentious demagogues, but no one seems to be offering any real opposition. If he attempts even a fraction of the things he has promised, Germany will become the leper of Europe. It will be worse than if socialists like your brother Walter came to power."

"Don't bring Walter into this. We never see him because you two always argued about politics. Yes, he is a socialist, but he is a kind man. You argue with him because you, Ernst Hammer, are an old-fashioned snob. You look down on everyone who is not an aristocrat and never owned estates in Prussia. You look down on Walter because he runs a pig farm and his father was a cobbler. He was my father, too."

"Yes," Ernst admitted, "but I love you. I don't love Walter — he smells too much of his precious pigs. And the reason we don't see Walter is because he refuses to leave his beloved sty and come to the city. Besides, this isn't about Walter, but about our new Chancellor.

"Eva," Ernst went on in a gentle voice so unlike his usual gruff tone that Dieter looked up from his soldiers. "Would you please think again about going to Canada?"

Dieter shot a glance at his mother. She was looking at her knitting, but her brow was furrowed with concentration as she listened to Ernst.

"I think, now that these people are solidly in power, that we need to make a decision. I keep remembering the pictures that Allen Shardlow sent at Christmas. The snow on the trees and the empty landscape remind me of the old estates in Prussia. Yes, you tease me, and I know I was just a boy when it was sold, but it is part of me nonetheless. I think we could be happy in Canada. It would be a new start — for the boys and for us. Allen would help us get settled, he said as much in his letter, and there are places where there are many German immigrants. I am afraid, Eva. Afraid of the way our country is going. Of where it will end. Of where the whole of Europe will end. The old values count for nothing anymore, and without them, we will drift wherever those thugs take us. Furthermore, our money is running out. We can barely afford to pay Elsa and —"

"Do you know why our money is running out?" Eva was now looking across at Ernst, determination in her eyes.

"The stock market crash —"

"Yes, the crash hurt," Eva interrupted. "And so did the Kaiser's war and inflation — I have heard it all before. You blame everything and everyone but yourself. You are almost thirty-seven, yet you still only have a minor post at the ministry. Your school friends have all advanced much higher. Why?

"Because," Eva answered her own question, "you live in the past. You say life was wonderful on the family estates. Maybe so, but they are long gone. This is a different world. You are pig-headed, Ernst Hammer, and you criticize every little thing you disagree with. That is why you are always passed over for promotion."

Eva fell silent and looked down at her knitting again.

"You may be right," Ernst said quietly. "I know many of my views are old-fashioned and not popular. But it is hard not to speak out when I see stupidity. I shall try to find more tolerance. But this does not answer my question: should we go to Canada?"

"No," Eva said simply.

"Why not?"

Eva lifted her eyes once more. This time, there was sadness in them. "I am sure Canada is a lovely country. And Mr. Shardlow is very kind to offer his help. I could just say that such a huge move, especially now that I am pregnant again, would be too disruptive, or that the economic depression is much worse in Canada than here, or that we cannot afford it and would end up penniless. All of these are true, but they are not the real reason."

Eva fell silent, and Ernst waited patiently. "I'm scared," she said at last. "Scared of leaving all that we have here, our friends, family, everything that is familiar. But mostly I am scared of becoming root-less. Yes, I am sure there are places in Canada where many from our country have settled, but that is the very problem. There are also areas that must be Italian and Greek and Japanese. Canada is a mongrel country. A land of immigrants who have exchanged countless generations of their heritage — for what? More security? A wealthier life? But is it worth it? I do not want our children to grow up not knowing who they are or who their people are.

"I do not like this man Hitler any more than you do, but he will pass. We are the people of Goethe and Beethoven. We will not allow the terrible things you fear. We are all Germans — even the Jews, despite the awful things the Nazis say. That will protect us in the long run, and we will always have our roots to comfort us." Eva smiled ruefully. "Perhaps I am just as conservative as you."

Dieter glanced from Eva to Ernst and back as they sat looking at each other.

"Very well," Ernst said eventually. "We will stay for the time being. I just pray you are right."

Dieter felt uneasy. Something important had happened, but he wasn't sure what. All this talk of moving and strange places and the intensity of his parents' words unsettled him, but he didn't know how to clear it up in his mind. At length, his attention was drawn back to Rajah. The tiger still had some soldiers to deal with.

"Tiger!" Joe shouted, suddenly alert again at the mention of Dieter's old toy. "We showed that old Tiger, didn't we, Tom?"

Joe stared hard at Dieter.

"It was just a toy," Dieter said. Joe's gaze drifted away.

"Why are you talking about your old toys?" Greta asked in a tired voice.

"I'm trying to keep Joe awake. I'm afraid he'll die if he goes to sleep. Then he won't be able to help us get to Canada."

"Oh," Greta said uninterestedly. "So we're not going to walk anymore now?"

"No," Dieter said. "Why don't you get some sleep?"

"All right." Greta huddled on the slope, and Dieter arranged his jacket over her. Then he turned back to Joe.

It was the second of May 1935. Dieter was sitting in front of the fire reading a story about a brave National Socialist boy who had saved his town by discovering a Communist cell and denouncing it to the authorities. Reinhard had given him the book that day for his seventh birthday, but Dieter was bored with it. He much preferred tales of cowboys and Indians, but they seemed difficult to come by.

"Why can't we get good, exciting books anymore?" he asked his father.

Ernst looked up from his newspaper. "Because our government is deciding what books are good and what are not. They burn books written by people they do not agree with."

"Reinhard says we must burn deco ... decu ... decadent books so that we will become pure."

"Books are treasures," Ernst said. "Even your exciting cowboy and war stories."

Dieter looked hard at his father. "Was it exciting in your war?" he asked.

"The war was many things," Ernst replied seriously. "It was terrifying, exhausting, boring and, yes, sometimes it was exciting. It is strange. War is terrible, and yet good things can come out of it. I made friends in the war I have valued all my life. One of them was even an enemy."

"Who was that?" Dieter asked, intrigued.

Ernst looked down at his son. "You know, one of the most difficult things in a war is to remember that the enemy is men just like yourself. They may have different uniforms and speak a different language, but underneath that, they are just as hungry and tired and scared.

"For years in the trenches I never thought of the enemy as people like us — until one day in 1918. It was the early morning of August 8. My unit was in the line south of Villers-Bretonneux, near Amiens in France. We had captured the town in the spring, but the Australians had taken it back in a night attack. For months, all had been quiet. The Canadians across from us seemed content just to sit.

"So the bombardment came as a complete surprise. It began at 4:20 in the morning — I know because it stopped my watch. It was like a hurricane. I had been through many bombardments, but nothing like this. The earth seemed alive, jumping and shaking like a wild beast. Our dugouts were deep, but we were thrown out of our beds by the concussion of the shells. It was impossible to stand. All we could do was dig our fingers into the earth and try to hold on.

"The bombardment didn't last long before moving on to our second line, but it left us absolutely stunned. We stumbled up the dugout steps into what was left of our trench, just as the Canadian assault troops arrived. They were highly trained and followed the barrage so closely that some men were killed by their own shells falling short. They arrived before we had time to set up our machine guns.

"Several small, vicious, hand-to-hand fights raged around me. We were outnumbered, but determined to fight as hard as we could. A tall soldier came at me brandishing a wicked-looking club. I lunged at him and, although he side-stepped, I caught him in his upper left arm with my bayonet. He roared and swung his club, which caught me on the side of the head, knocking my helmet off.

"I was dazed — I think I passed out for a second or two. The next thing I remembered was this man standing over me. His left arm hung useless and bloodstained where I had stabbed him. He had his club raised to crush my skull and he was cursing wildly. I closed my eyes, expecting to die.

"When I opened them, the man had stopped cursing and was staring at my chest. When the bombardment started, I hadn't had time to get dressed — I had simply thrown on my tunic and grabbed my rifle. I was engaged to your mother and always kept her photograph in my pocket as a good luck charm. She was eighteen and very beautiful.

"When I fell, the photograph must have slipped from my pocket. It lay on my chest — that was what the man was looking at. The picture changed the way he saw me — it made me a human being. Perhaps it reminded him of someone at home. In any case, he gestured for me to stand up.

"The fighting had stopped, and the Canadians had won. There were a number of bodies, but most of my company were standing about with their hands in the air. The barrage and most of the Canadians had moved on. All that were left were a handful of wounded and a few dead.

"We were afraid. We all knew that some men — on our side and theirs — had been killed while surrendering. Such things happen in the heat of battle. No one wanted to make a move that could be misinterpreted, so we all stood like statues, looking nervously at one another. It was my captor who broke the ice. Dropping his club, he reached into his tunic pocket and pulled out a pack of cigarettes. He offered me one and gestured that I should share them around, which I did. Then I took a field dressing and bandaged his arm.

"That was it. In only a few minutes, with simple gestures, we had changed from enemies to individuals.

"The wounded Canadians escorted us to the rear. On the way, the man I had bayoneted talked to me. His name was Allen Shardlow. He spoke a few words of German and I a few of English, so we got by. He told me of logging in the wilderness north of a town called Toronto, and of starting a farm on the prairies. I told him of my childhood in the Prussian forests and of Berlin.

"It was the strangest thing. We talked for only an hour or two, yet a strong connection grew between us. I suppose it was the release of tension after the battle, but it was no less real for that. Before we separated, we exchanged addresses. Then he went to a hospital and I to a prison camp. I never saw Allen again, but for many years we communicated by letter, usually at Christmas and when one of our children was born. We exchanged photographs. I was amazed at how much like Prussia Allen's part of Canada looked. He even invited us to go to Canada — he would help us get a start if we wanted to emigrate. I was quite keen, but your mother — well, it didn't happen.

"It's ridiculous, really, that a single morning should have left me with such a strong feeling for an entire country. Allen Shardlow was no more representative of Canadians than I am of Germans, yet I have always wanted to visit him and see his country. I don't suppose I ever shall now.

"Anyway, there are two things I want you to remember from my story. First, whatever people are like and whatever they do that you like or don't agree with, we are all human. That is a simple thing to say, but difficult to remember when you are very angry. Second, when you are grown up, if you need to leave Germany, Canada would be a good place to go."

Ernst ruffled Dieter's hair. "Sorry," he said, "I didn't mean to get so serious — and on your birthday!"

"It's the best birthday ever," Dieter said, feeling very grown-up having his father talk to him about serious things, even if he didn't understand them all.

"Good," Ernst replied, pulling himself up from his chair. "Let's go and see if Elsa has got our supper ready."

✦ ✦ ✦

"We're going to the Olympics!" Reinhard gleefully announced on the last day of July 1936.

"We couldn't get tickets for the opening tomorrow — they were sold out — but we got

..." Reinhard paused for dramatic effect, "... the long-jump final."

Dieter was thrilled. Luz Long was one of his heroes and now he would see him in the Olympics. Long was Germany's hope to break the world record held by the American Jesse Owens.

The next week, the family made their way to the Olympic Stadium — except for three-year-old Greta, who stayed home with Elsa. Reinhard strutted in his Jungvolk uniform — it had been allowed for this special occasion — and chattered nonstop. "That degenerate black will get his comeuppance today."

Ernst appeared about to say something, but Dieter got in first. "How can he be degenerate? Owens has won two gold medals already."

"In running," Reinhard said dismissively. "The Aryan strengths are in the manly sports — boxing, discus, javelin — and the technical ones, equestrian and gymnastics. Anyone with long legs can run fast."

"And anyone with strong arms can fling a javelin," Ernst muttered. If Reinhard heard, he ignored his father. At fourteen, he had learned all about Nazi racial theory in school and at his youth group.

"Let's not argue," Eva said. "It's going to be a beautiful day, and I just want to see the sports."

"Mother! You can't ignore —" Reinhard began, but a stern look from Ernst silenced him.

The stadium was magnificent. From the entrance between the twin towers, through the forest of pillars around the circumference of the huge circle, to the thousands of seats surrounding the playing field, the place was covered in blood-red flags and black swastikas. Across from where Dieter sat was the covered special-visitors section. In the center, Reinhard breathlessly pointed out, sat Adolf Hitler himself, surrounded by uniformed politicians and officials. The few Olympic officials in civilian clothes looked distinctly uncomfortable.

"Hitler walked out when Owens won the one-hundred and two-hundred-meters races," Reinhard said.

"Atrocious manners," Ernst grumbled, but further debate was prevented by a fanfare of trumpets. It was time for the long jump. The athletes milled around the pit. Owens, the first black man Dieter had ever seen, stood out dramatically beside the blond Long. A hush fell as the athletes prepared for their qualifying jumps. Each had three attempts to reach the final by beating 7.15 meters. For Owens and Long, it would be no problem. Owens's world record was almost a meter better than that, and Long had jumped nearly as far.

Still in his track suit, Owens sprinted down the runway but pulled up short.

"What's he doing?" Dieter asked.

"Testing the run up," Ernst said. "It doesn't count."

"Yes it does!" Reinhard shouted triumphantly. "The flags are up for a foul jump."

"That's ridiculous," Ernst exclaimed. "He was obviously not jumping."

"Doesn't matter." Reinhard grinned. "He has two qualifying jumps left."

Long qualified on his first jump. To avoid a foul by overstepping the line, he had placed his towel on the ground beside the track, well before the jumping board. By jumping at the towel, he would qualify easily and not risk a foul.

Owens came up for his second attempt. He was now stripped down to his white uniform with the red and blue diagonal stripes across the chest, but the unfair foul call had obviously unnerved him.

"Foul jump!" Reinhard shouted as the flags went up a second time.

Dieter was confused. If Owens failed a third time, nothing could stop his hero Long from winning gold. But it wasn't a very exciting way to do it. He watched intently as Long approached Owens and said something to him.

Then Long walked down the track and placed his towel in front of the jumping board.

"Long's helping him!" Dieter exclaimed. "Look, he's putting down his towel the way he did for himself."

"Well, well. So he is." Ernst chuckled. "There's some sportsmanship left in the world after all."

Owens qualified comfortably on his third attempt.

In the final, the lead changed between the two athletes with each jump. After four jumps for Owens and five for Long, both men had leaped 7.87 meters. Owens had one jump left. If he jumped farther, he would win gold.

The stadium was silent as Owens stared down the runway. Then with long, loping strides, he was off, speed building until he planted a foot and leaped. To Dieter, Owens appeared to hang in the air forever. Reinhard sat beside Dieter, his face a mask of concentration. Dieter knew Reinhard was wishing for Owens to fail. But it was such a beautiful sight, Dieter didn't mind if he won.

The officials scurried to mark and measure the jump. After what seemed like an age, the result was posted: 8.06 meters. A new Olympic record and another gold-medal performance. The international crowd erupted in a frenzy of cheering.

The first man to shake Owens's hand was Luz Long. Arm in arm, the two best long jumpers in the world jogged onto the track and past Hitler's box for a lap of honor. The box was empty.

"Long is a real gentleman," Ernst stated. "Brave, too. It took courage to walk arm in arm with Owens in front of Hitler's box."

"But Hitler isn't there," Dieter pointed out.

"He will hear about it," Ernst said. "And when he does, he will be very angry with Long. But it's good to see that fanatic's crazy ideas turned on their heads. Good for Jesse Owens, and good for Luz Long."

+ + +

"Look, little brother." Reinhard barged into Dieter's room. He was waving two booklets. "This is what I was telling you about the other day — degenerate art." He handed one of them to Dieter. The cover was a photograph of a grotesque head in rough stone. The lips were wide, the nose large and the eyebrows prominent. It reminded Dieter of a primitive idol. "What is it?" he asked.

"It's the catalog from an exhibition in Munich. The Führer has put all the worst pieces of art from the museums in Germany in one exhibition hall so people can see how low so-called modern art has sunk. It's a stroke of genius. Now everyone will see how our culture is being undermined. Look at this trash."

Dieter thumbed through the book. Some of the pictures were of nothing at all, just lines and colors. Others showed recognizable things, but oddly drawn, with facial features in the wrong place and arms and legs suddenly turning into flowers. Some just looked like the scrawls little Greta made with her crayons. Dieter felt vaguely unsettled. Even the names of the artists were strange and foreign — Kandinsky, Chagall, Picasso, Klee.

"What does 'surrealist' mean?" Dieter asked.

"Who knows. None of this garbage means anything."

Dieter was strangely drawn to the surrealist paintings. Figures had no faces or were built out of machine parts. Perfectly drawn pianos or clocks were set in deserts or buildings with walls missing. Dark landscapes appeared to be ruined cities, but when he looked closer, they turned out to be growths of nature. They were confusing, but Dieter couldn't tear his eyes away from the images. They were mesmerizing.

"Dreadful, isn't it?" Reinhard snorted. "It's hard to believe people have been fooled by these

charlatans. But here's another stroke of genius —
there's another exhibition right across the road
from this degenerate nonsense, so people can see
what *real* art is."

Reinhard pushed the second booklet into
Dieter's hands. The portraits of people and landscapes had no unnatural objects in them. They
were easy to understand. They all made sense.
They all looked real. Dieter handed Reinhard the
second catalog, but he kept looking at the pictures in the first one.

"I don't much like those modern pictures
either." Ernst's voice came from the doorway.
"An interesting thing, though. Apparently the
degenerate art is crammed into small, dark
rooms and the official art is displayed in a brand-
new gallery."

"As it should be," Reinhard said.

"Maybe," Ernst went on thoughtfully. "But
three times as many people are visiting the
degenerate gallery." With a puff on his pipe,
Ernst continued down the corridor.

"He doesn't understand," Reinhard said petulantly, grabbing the catalog and heading to his
own room.

Dieter thought it over. He had felt comfortable
with the "real" art, but it was the surreal images
that stayed in his mind. Odd.

+ + +

It was a Thursday morning, November 10, 1938, and the three children were walking hand in hand along the broad pavement toward school. Ahead of them, columns of black smoke drifted up from the still-smoldering remains of Berlin's largest synagogues. It was Reinhard's seventeenth birthday, but he didn't look happy.

"These are extraordinary times," he grumbled. "Why can't Father see that? How could he have kept me from the special Hitler Youth meeting?"

Ernst had suspected there might be trouble in the streets — and he'd been right. All night, the family had heard shouts and screams, running feet and shattering glass. Reinhard had missed out on history in the making.

On Monday, von Rath, Third Secretary of the German Embassy in Paris, had been shot by a Jewish teenager whose family had been deported to Poland. On Wednesday, von Rath had died. Nazis all over Germany had taken to the streets, burning synagogues, shattering the windows of Jewish shops and attacking Jews in the street. The radio said that more than ninety Jews had been killed.

"We can't ignore the Jewish murderers," Reinhard said, his voice heavy with righteous indignation. "Last night was a spontaneous reaction to their scheming. Should red-blooded Aryans sit back and watch good Germans get killed in cold blood? No. The Jews brought it on themselves."

Ten-year-old Dieter thought hard about what Reinhard was saying. His world had changed a great deal in the two years since the Olympics. He had watched with pride as Greater Germany had grown to include the Rhineland, Austria and, just a month ago, the Sudetenland. Surely all the German people in these places had a right to be part of their own country.

From listening to his father, Dieter also knew that it had become dangerous to speak out against Hitler and the Nazis — if you did, you were sent to something called a concentration camp. But Dieter had never met anyone who had been to a concentration camp, so it didn't mean much.

And why would anyone say bad things about Hitler? Dieter's comics, books, radio, all told him what wonderful things Hitler was doing for Germany — the economy was thriving, everyone had work, the army was strong again. At school the teacher stood beneath a huge painting of Hitler looking very handsome and strong and told the children that they must be ready for the great future that awaited them. Movies showed huge rallies of soldiers, ranks of strong men and beautiful women smiling as they worked in the fields and factories, and horrible-looking, hooked-nosed Jews swindling and cheating hard-working Germans — so it must be true, just as Reinhard kept telling him. But Ernst argued that Hitler and the others were just low-class thugs who fed gullible people simplistic propaganda.

Dieter's emotions were in turmoil. Partly he agreed with his father, but it was much easier to go along with everyone else. Occasionally, as he lay awake in the darkness listening to the some-times violent noises on the street outside, Dieter's doubts welled up. Who was right — his father or his brother?

Dieter had tried to talk to Reinhard about it, but his brother had simply laughed. "You're too young to understand — and Father is too old." But some-thing he had said this morning seemed odd.

"What does 'spontaneous' mean, Reinhard?" Dieter asked.

"It means instinctively, without thinking about it first. Like last night. People had had enough of Jewish tricks, so they took matters into their own hands. No one planned it, it just happened."

"If something's spontaneous," Dieter went on, "do you know it's going to happen?"

"No, of course not."

"Well," Dieter's brow furrowed as he tried to formulate his question, "if last night was spontaneous, how come you got a phone call to go to the special meeting before we'd even had supper?"

"You're too young to understand," Reinhard said again as they rounded the corner to Greta's school. The street was covered in the glass from three large windows, leaving the shops behind them open like gaping wounds. Papers, Hebrew prayer books and goods from the shops lay scattered and trampled all over the road. On the sidewalk, a blackened pile was all that was left of bolts of colored cloth. The walls of Rothstein's Drapery shop were painted with the word "JEW" and crude drawings of big-nosed men with their hair in ringlets. The red paint ran down from the letters, making Dieter think the walls were bleeding.

A handbill pasted on the door read "The Jews are undermining our glorious march to the future. Germans! Defend yourselves against the Jewish Conspiracy!"

Rothstein's Drapery was where Dieter's mother bought fabric for the children's clothes. Every time Dieter and Greta went there with their mother, Mrs. Rothstein gave them candy. Now Greta pulled her hand out of Dieter's and ran toward a middle-aged woman in a shapeless print dress, sweeping up glass and papers.

"Mrs. Rothstein!" she shouted. "What happened? Where's Mr. Rothstein and Marcus? Why did your window break?"

The woman looked up just in time to brace herself against Greta's hug.

"It's all right, dear," she said. "Some bad people came last night and broke our window, but we are fine. David and Marcus have gone to help clean up the synagogue."

Marcus was a quiet, studious boy who wore rimless glasses. He was the only Jewish student in Dieter's class — all the others had left to go to Jewish schools.

Dieter and Marcus had played together a few times when they'd been little — before it was illegal — but school life was hard for Marcus. He was always being bullied — even the teacher picked on him, making him stand at the front of the class as an example of a "degenerate Jew."

Marcus never complained and never fought back, trying to blend in. This was difficult because he looked Jewish. He didn't have the exaggerated features of the comics or the ringlets that Dieter sometimes saw on Orthodox Jews in the street, but his olive complexion and prominent nose drew attention.

"Why don't you fight back, Marcus?" Dieter had asked him once after Marcus had been pushed into the mud by one of the class bullies.

"Because if I do," Marcus had explained, "the whole class will gang up on me and my life will become even worse. It is better to try to be invisible."

This didn't help Dieter understand. Wasn't it always better to fight back? Were the bullies right when they called Marcus a coward? Part of him felt guilty about not helping Marcus, but even talking to him openly would trigger jibes of "Jew lover" and make Dieter a target, too. Dieter wished Marcus would solve the problem by going to a Jewish school.

Most of the time, Dieter managed to push his dilemma out of his mind, but it was back now as he felt Reinhard's hand on his shoulder. Dieter wanted to help Mrs. Rothstein clean up the mess, but his brother's message was clear. So he stood and watched as Greta and the woman talked. Just then, an open truck swerved around the corner, the back full of boys in Hitler Youth uniforms. One of the boys was Reinhard's friend Alfred.

"Hey, Reinhard!" Alfred shouted. "You missed all the fun last night. Don't get too close to that Jewess. You might catch the Jew disease." Then the truck was gone in a swirl of laughter.

"Damn!" Stepping hurriedly forward, Reinhard grabbed Greta roughly by the arm.

"Greta," he said harshly, "get away from that Jew swine."

Dragging the surprised Greta by the arm, Reinhard strode toward the school. Mrs. Rothstein looked up at Dieter, her face calm but unutterably sad.

"Sorry," Dieter mumbled, lowering his eyes and crunching his way over the glass shards, angry and ashamed.

A rumbling hum interrupted Dieter's story. Instinctively, he switched off his flashlight.

"What?" Joe said weakly. "What is it?"

"It's all right," Dieter responded reassuringly. "Bombers heading east. They are high. They won't see us." As he spoke, a searchlight pierced the darkness far to the north. Almost immediately, it was answered by colored flares dropping slowly from the pathfinder bombers. Then came the high explosives, distant crumps that coagulated into a continuous deep thumping that was felt as much as heard.

"Tiger! Tiger!" Joe shouted excitedly.

"No, it's not," Dieter said, placing a hand reassuringly on Joe's shoulder. "It's just the bombs
landing over there." He pointed to the flickering
lights on the horizon.

Dieter was feeling anxious. His storytelling
was keeping Joe alert and alive — that was good;
but it was also bringing memories. Not just
images of happier times, but complex feelings
that Dieter had pushed into the back of his mind.

"Sure are pretty fireworks over there, eh,
Tom?" Joe was straining to look at the bombing.
"Must be one helluva party, eh? Wish we could
go to a party, Tom. Find ourselves a drink, dance
with some pretty girls."

Greta turned over in her sleep, and Dieter
readjusted his jacket over her.

"We used to have good parties," Dieter said.
Joe was still gazing at the distant searchlights
and flares. "Father knew some important people,
and Mother would put on quite a spread. Of
course, it got harder as the war went on and the
bombing got worse, but there was always some
treat or other on the table."

Dieter didn't know if Joe was listening, but it
didn't matter. He was telling the story as much
for himself as for Joe. His mind was filled with
images of sparkling parties in their flat's high-
ceilinged parlor. Dieter and Greta used to slip out

of bed and sit in the shadows at the end of the long corridor, watching the comings and goings. Occasionally, Elsa would sneak the children goodies from the kitchen. Greta oohed and aahed at the women's beautiful gowns and sparkling jewels, while Dieter silently watched the men in their formal dress or army uniforms and medals. They all looked so self-assured, talking to one another with the beautiful women on their arms — just the way Dieter wanted to be one day.

After the war began, Ernst and Eva's parties changed. There were more uniforms and more men huddled in serious conversation. Not that anyone was downcast. After all, the Panzers had rolled through Poland, Holland, Denmark, Luxembourg, Belgium, Norway, France, Greece and Yugoslavia. Europe belonged to Germany, just as Hitler had promised, and that was something to be proud of. But Dieter detected a new undertone, especially after the first bombing raids by the British air force. The raids were small and did little damage — the radio said most of the bombers were shot down — but Hitler had promised that Berlin would never be attacked. The blackout, the camouflage netting strung over the streets and the huge, concrete anti-aircraft Flak Towers in the Tiergarten were constant reminders that he'd been wrong.

As the summer of 1941 began, Dieter noticed another change — there were no uniforms at his parents' parties. Then came news of the invasion of Russia — the Panzers had rolled east as effortlessly as they had rolled west the previous year. True, winter had stopped them just outside Moscow, but next summer would see the end of Russia, too.

Reinhard finished his training that fall and was ecstatic at having been accepted into the Leibstandarte Adolf Hitler, the First Waffen SS Panzer Division, victors in the battles in Poland, France and Russia. Reinhard considered his posting a great honor and Dieter was thrilled for him. When Reinhard had arrived home after six months' training, pride shone right through him.

Dieter and Greta had been putting the finishing touches on the tree when the doorbell rang. They leaped to their feet and scrambled against each other in their eagerness to be the one to open the door. Dieter flung the heavy door wide. And there he was. At twenty years old, Reinhard had grown to almost two meters tall and he was at the peak of fitness.

"Wow! You look great," Dieter said. Reinhard straightened his already straight cap as his brother stared. Reinhard's dark blue-gray uniform was immaculately pressed, the perfect background for the runic "SS" on the right collar, the double bars of rank on the left, the eagle and swastika on the chest and the death's head on the cap.

"What does that one mean?" Dieter asked, pointing to the left collar.

"That's my rank badge," Reinhard replied. "We have our own ranks in the SS. I am an oberschutze — that would be a private first class in the army. And look," he went on, raising his left cuff for examination. Around it was a black band with the words "Adolf Hitler." "We are the only Division allowed to wear the Führer's name. We are his favorites. Just like the Praetorian Guard were the favorites of the Caesars."

"Wow!" Dieter repeated.

"Thank you, Little Brother," Reinhard said with a click of his heels, "but may I come in?"

"What? Oh, of course," Dieter stuttered as he stepped aside, pulling the equally awestruck Greta with him.

Reinhard placed his brown leather case beside the hat stand in the hall. "Aren't you going to wish me a Merry Christmas?" he asked teasingly.

Greta flung herself at her brother. "Merry, merry Christmas!" she shouted. Reinhard lifted her effortlessly and swung her around. "Merry Christmas to you, too," he said, laughing. Then he put her down and shook hands formally with Dieter. "Merry Christmas, Little Brother," he said. "Have you been looking after everyone?"

Dieter nodded.

Reinhard raised his head over Dieter. "Hello, Father." Dieter turned to see Ernst standing at the parlor door. Ruffling Dieter's hair, Reinhard stepped past him and held out his hand. Dieter thought he detected some hesitation by his father, but the pair shook hands cordially enough and exchanged Christmas greetings.

"Welcome home, Reinhard," Ernst said. "Why not take your case to your room and change for dinner? Elsa has done us proud this year with the goose."

Reinhard looked over his shoulder. "Bring my suitcase, Little Brother," he said.

Dieter grabbed the case, and he and Greta followed Reinhard along the corridor.

Reinhard's room was a shrine to the new Germany. The walls were covered with posters showing bare-chested, fit young men exercising, working or gazing determinedly to the future. Photographs recorded the huge rallies at

Nuremberg, cheering crowds welcoming German troops into Austria and stern portraits of Hitler and other Nazi leaders. Reinhard glanced around at the walls, took the suitcase from Dieter and tossed it on the bed. "I've brought you a present," he said. "You might want to open it here … rather than in front of Father."

"Me too, me too," Greta squawked excitedly.

"Be patient." Reinhard laughed. "I've brought something for you too."

From beneath his pressed clothes, Reinhard withdrew a flat package. Dieter tore off the wrapping — maybe it was a book. But it turned out to be a framed photograph. The frame was silver and embossed with German eagles and swastikas. The photograph was of a soldier in three-quarter profile and wearing the uniform of a high-ranking officer. His face was stern and his jaw firm. His expression said "Don't oppose me. You'll get the worst of it."

Across the bottom was scrawled "Best wishes, Sepp Dietrich."

Dieter fought to not let his puzzlement and disappointment show. But Reinhard chattered on enthusiastically. "General der Waffen SS, Sepp Dietrich. He is the commander of the Leibstandarte. He is one of Hitler's closest friends and a brilliant commander. See?" Reinhard pointed at the photograph. "He has the Iron Cross First Class with an Oak Leaves Cluster. He fought in the First World War, too, just like Father. He reviewed us when we graduated. The photograph is signed in his own hand. When you are old enough, you can join the Leibstandarte, too."

Dieter didn't know what to say. Obviously, the photograph was important to Reinhard, and Dieter was flattered by the gift, but he would rather have had an exciting book or a toy.

Luckily, he was saved by Greta blurting out, "I hope you didn't get me a crummy old photograph."

"No," Reinhard chuckled. "The photographs are just for soldiers. German womenfolk have to prepare the homeland for the returning heroes. This is what I got for you."

He made a big show of rummaging around in his suitcase as Greta danced impatiently from one foot to the other. Eventually, Reinhard produced a small elongated package. Greta eagerly tore off the paper. "A doll!" she squeaked. "She's beautiful. Thank you."

The doll wore bright peasant costume. She was smiling and her face radiated health and beauty. Long straw-colored hair flowed to her waist, and over her arm hung a basket of fruit and vegetables. On her upper right arm was a red band sporting a black swastika.

"I shall call her Ingrid," Greta said as she disappeared to introduce her new friend to her old toys.

"Yes, thank you," Dieter said, when Greta was gone.

"You're welcome. You know, Dieter, the last six months have been the best in my life. At last I feel I am doing something for the greater good of Germany, and I've been with others who feel the same. It's a wonderful feeling. I hope you feel it one day, too."

"I hope so."

"It is a bit strange to come home," Reinhard went on. "There is such a feeling of belonging in the unit, of common purpose. It's a feeling I never had here. Oh, I love Mother and Father and you and Greta, but Father is so stuffy. He doesn't appreciate the wonderful things that are happening."

Reinhard stood straighter and raised his right arm in the Nazi salute. "We pledge to you, Adolf Hitler, loyalty and bravery. We swear obedience to you and the superiors appointed by you, even unto death, as God is our witness." He lowered his arm. "That is our pledge when we are accepted into the SS."

"Let me show you something." Reinhard removed his jacket and rolled up his left shirt sleeve. On the inside of his arm, above the elbow, were some blue letters and numbers.

"Is that a tattoo?" Dieter asked.

"Everyone in the SS has one."

"What does it mean?"

"It's my blood group," Reinhard said proudly. "If one of our unit is wounded, the doctor doesn't need to do any tests to make sure a blood transfusion will work — he just has to look at our arms."

"Does it come off?"

"Not unless I burn all the skin off."

"Father will be furious!" Dieter said. "He says tattoos are only for sailors and other riffraff."

"Then we'd better not tell him," Reinhard said with a smile as he rolled down his sleeve and put his jacket back on. "But I haven't told you the big news yet."

"What?" Dieter asked.

"I am to be posted east to fight the Russians. There won't be much action before the spring, but then I shall be a part of the great final offensive. Nineteen-forty-two is going to be a great year."

Images of his brother sitting triumphantly on a Panzer as it rolled victoriously over the steppes rushed around Dieter's mind. His own brother, making history!

"I leave straight from here after Christmas," Reinhard said as Greta burst in to tell them that their presence was requested in the dining room and to announce proudly that there would be a flute recital after the meal. Reinhard buttoned his jacket.

"You're not sitting down to dinner in your uniform?" Greta was horrified.

"Why not?" Reinhard asked. "We should all be proud of this uniform."

"But you know how Father feels about it."

"He will just have to get used to it," Reinhard said, and stepped into the hall.

Greta was right. Ernst was not happy to see Reinhard in his uniform, but he said nothing, confining himself to a disapproving look. Christmas dinner went well until Reinhard marched off after his argument with Ernst. Later, when Dieter was in his room in tears, Ernst knocked softly on his door. Dieter refused to answer, but Ernst entered and sat on the edge of his son's bed.

"That unpleasantness was my fault," he said. "Your mother says that I should not have taken him to task. Reinhard has some strong views that I disagree with, but Christmas dinner is not the time or place to discuss them. I sometimes take what he says too seriously — everything is either black or white, every answer obvious. I forget that he is still a boy with no experience of life. But I am sorry you were caught in the middle."

Sniffling, Dieter lifted his tearstained face and looked at his father. "He's going to Russia."

"I thought he would," Ernst said sadly. "Best not to mention it to Mother. She will find out in good time, but she is already upset over the mess I made of her lovely dinner."

"Why do you hate Reinhard so?"

"Hate Reinhard? I don't hate Reinhard. He is my son. I love him dearly. It's just that I don't like the people he admires and I worry about the decisions he is making."

"But Hitler has done so much for us, and the war is going so well."

"True," Ernst admitted. "The economy is better than it has been since before the First War. We have wonderful new roads and buildings, and German pride has certainly been restored. But the cost has been high. Hitler's opponents are all in prison, and we are in the midst of a vast war —"

"That we will win," Dieter interrupted.

"Possibly," Ernst said. "But a year ago, we were just fighting Britain. Now we are at war with Russia and America, too. If we don't beat Russia very quickly next year, I fear the war will drag on, and that will not be good for us."

"We will beat them," Dieter said. "Especially with Reinhard there to help."

Ernst stroked his son's head. "Let's hope so. Now, go and join your mother and Greta. I must make my peace with Reinhard. We can't have him going off to beat the Russians angry at me, can we?"

Reinhard rejoined the family in time to applaud Greta's flute repertoire of folk tunes, but the atmosphere was very strained. Neither he nor Ernst said much. The next morning, Reinhard left early, before the rest of the family was awake.

+ + +

The following summer, as the German army was again rolling east across the Russian Steppes, Dieter squirmed uncomfortably in the heat in his brand-new black Hitler Youth uniform. On the flag-decked podium, uniformed dignitaries watched as the sun beat down on lines of boys receiving tokens of their new status as full Hitler Youth members. Proud families cheered each inductee. Carefully, Dieter scanned the new arrivals at the back of the crowd. There was no sign of his parents.

Dieter knew that Ernst didn't approve of his uniform any more than he had of Reinhard's, but now that membership in the Hitler Youth was compulsory, he thought it unfair that his parents had stayed away. Besides, Dieter loved the youth movement. In his uniform, with his friends, there was always something to do — camping trips and war games in the woods around Berlin, boating on the Rhine, tours of factories producing massive tanks and guns, and work clearing away bomb damage.

The raids were still small. The radio proclaimed that the bombers did little damage and most were destroyed, but, despite the searchlights and anti-aircraft fire, bombs did fall. A few days earlier, Dieter and his best friend, Karl, had been clearing a pile of rubble that had been a house. It was hard work, loading bricks into wheelbarrows and taking them to the waiting trucks, but the boys kept up a constant chatter.

"This is nothing compared to what the Luftwaffe did to London," Karl said.

"Or what the RAF did to Cologne," Dieter countered. "They say there were a thousand bombers on that raid." Dieter didn't say who "they" were, but everyone would know. Even though it was illegal, many people listened to the BBC radio in the evenings. No one believed everything in the British broadcast, but it made an interesting contrast to what Propaganda Minister Goebbels was saying on German radio.

"That's just Churchill's propaganda," said Karl. "The British don't have a thousand bombers. Even if they did, the Luftwaffe would shoot them out of the sky like —"

Dieter turned to see why his friend had stopped speaking. Karl stood atop a pile of rubble, frozen in the act of lifting a broken slab of wall plaster.

"What is it?" Dieter asked. "What have you found?"

Karl pushed the plaster aside and together the boys gazed down. In the center of a hole in the rubble was a woman's foot, complete with high-heeled shoe and the tattered remnants of a silk stocking. It had been severed in a mass of torn, red flesh about mid-calf.

Dieter gasped. "Goebbels said no one was killed in the last raid." As if in answer, Karl retched into his wheelbarrow.

Even in the heat, Dieter shivered at the memory.

Karl, in line behind him, pushed Dieter in the back. "Come on, stop daydreaming."

Dieter mounted the steps to the podium. He searched the crowd one last time. Still no sign of his parents, but someone was waving. A figure in uniform at the back. Reinhard! Dieter smiled and stepped forward. His troop leader clicked his heels and snapped his arm up in a salute. Dieter copied him. The man handed him a small knife in a black leather scabbard, and — now it was Karl's turn. Dieter wanted to rush over to find Reinhard, but the ceremony wasn't finished yet — the oath was still to be taken.

Standing in rows, the new Hitler Youth faced the podium.

"You are the future of steel and destiny," the troop leader said. "All weakness has been hammered out. You are violent, masterful, intrepid, cruel, able to endure pain. You will be magnificent, free predators, unencumbered by thousands of years of human domestication. You are the noble raw material of nature. You will terrify the world.

"Your greatest achievement may be to die for Hitler before you are twenty. But is that not a wonderful privilege? What greater and more glorious mission can a German boy have than to die for the savior of Germany?

"And now raise your right hands and repeat after me the oath that will indeed make you Hitler's soldiers, ready to lay down your lives for him."

Dieter, Karl and the others raised their right hands and said in unison, "In the presence of this blood banner, which represents our Führer, I swear to devote all my energies and my strength to the savior of our country, Adolf Hitler. I am willing and ready to give up my life for him, so help me God."

Then they were done. Clutching his new dagger and not feeling much like a magnificent free predator, Dieter mumbled his excuses to Karl and ran to the back of the crowd. There was Reinhard, thinner than at Christmas, but just as handsome. Without thinking about his new dignity, Dieter flung himself at Reinhard. His brother looked surprised, but returned the hug.

Then, gently pushing Dieter away, he said, "So, Little Brother, you have your dagger now. Let's see it."

The handle protruded from the black scabbard. It too was black, but decorated with a red-and-white badge and a black swastika. Gently, Dieter pulled the blade from its sheath. The blade was wide and about the length of Dieter's hand. Along the middle, in swirling Gothic script, were engraved the words "Blood and Honor."

"That," said Reinhard, "must be your constant companion and most prized possession." He reached around his belt and produced an identical knife. "In the most desperate situations in Russia, I took my knife out and read the words on the blade. They gave me comfort."

"Did you beat the Communists?" Dieter asked excitedly. "When will our great advance to victory begin? Why are you back? How long are you here for?"

"Hold on. Hold on." Reinhard said, replacing his knife at his belt. "One question at a time. I am only here for a few hours — we are just passing through. The division is to be refitted in France. Mother said you would be here, so I thought I would come along and cheer. Let's go and —"

"You've been promoted!" Dieter cried, pointing at his brother's collar insignia. The SS runes were the same as before, but the two bars now had a silver dot beside them.

"Yes," Reinhard replied, "your brother is now a Scharführer, that would be a sergeant in the army. And," he went on proudly, "I am to be recommended for officer school this autumn. By Christmas, I could be a mighty Ünterstürmführer — second lieutenant to you.

"Now, let's go for a cup of coffee before I have to head back to the station."

The pair crossed the park and found an outdoor café. Dieter bathed in the admiring glances his brother drew from passersby. When they were seated, he returned to his questions. "What was Russia like?"

"Big," said Reinhard, laughing. "You can travel for hundreds of kilometers and it looks exactly the same as where you began — nothing but flat snow, like traveling over a blanket. And cold! It is too cold for machinery to work. Metal burns bare flesh. Everything freezes, even the hairs inside your nose."

Dieter tried to imagine that cold, but he couldn't. Having his fingers go numb because he'd forgotten his gloves was the worst he could come up with.

"Where were you?" he asked.

"Down in the south, near Rostov. We were dug in on the Mius River. All through January, February and March the Russians attacked, but we held."

"Did you kill any Russians?"

"Hundreds." Reinhard smiled. "They came at us in waves across the steppes. You couldn't miss. Once, they even attacked us with cavalry — maybe they thought they were still fighting Napoleon. The machine guns mowed them down.

"And the Luftwaffe! We would spot tanks concentrating for an attack and call in the planes. The Stukas would dive with their sirens blaring — they'd blow the tanks to bits before they even got moving. It was wonderful to see. The Russians don't have anything to match the Messerschmitt 109. It's the best fighter in the world. Our bombers can go where they please."

"I wish I'd been there."

"But it wasn't all easy." Reinhard was more serious now. "There was a lot of hard fighting — we had almost six thousand casualties in the division. That is why they pulled us out for a refit. It means we'll miss the big attack this month. It would have been so good to go forward after being stuck in the same place all winter. But we need new equipment and a rest — von Paulus and the Sixth Army can have the glory this summer. Our turn will come."

"But the war will be over by fall," Dieter said.

Reinhard shrugged. "Perhaps. They say the Russians are on their last legs, but I don't know. Russia is a vast place, and even the areas we have conquered are not completely secure. Our supplies often didn't make it through to us because of partisans operating in the woods behind us. We caught some of them — hanged them in the villages as a warning — but it didn't seem to make much difference. The Jews and the Communists have had a long time to get their talons into the people."

"Are the Jews being resettled from Russia, like they are from Berlin?"

"Resettled? Yes, of course they are being resettled. But never mind the Jews. How are things here in Berlin?" Reinhard asked, changing the subject abruptly.

"Fine," Dieter replied. "We are kept awake some nights by the bombers, but the anti-aircraft guns send them packing. There is talk of moving down to the cellar at nights, but no bombs have landed close to us. It is all just a nuisance."

"How is Father?"

"He is well. He enjoys reading your letters to Mother, although he still looks on the dark side. Why can't he be hopeful? These are such positive times. He barely says a word to me anymore, and he never plays with Greta."

"I saw Greta at the house. She seems cheerful."

"Oh yes. Greta will always be cheerful. She's in the Junior Hitler Youth now — loves dressing up in peasant costume and learning the old folk dances. She also loves Ingrid — that doll you gave her. It never leaves her side."

"That reminds me," Reinhard said, reaching into his tunic pocket. "I missed your birthday. I got you a present."

For a moment Dieter worried that it might be another photograph, but the package Reinhard handed him was much too small. Inside was a metal disk. On one side was a soldier aiming a rifle, and on the other, a bright red enamel star.

"It's a Russian medal," Reinhard explained. "I don't know what it's for, but I got it off a prisoner — he must have been close to sixty. They send old men and boys against us now. That is how desperate they are."

Dieter examined the medal closely. It was beautiful. "Thank you, Reinhard. Wait till I show it to Karl. He'll be so jealous!"

"Perhaps one day soon, you can join the SS and capture your own Russian. But I must get back to the station now." Reinhard stood. "Say hello to Father for me. Have fun and keep out of the way of the bombs."

Dieter stood for a long time, watching his brother march towards the railway station.

"I got rid of the medal some time ago," Dieter explained to Joe. "It didn't seem very smart to carry a Russian medal around with me. But I still have the knife. Do you want to see it?"

Joe made no sign, but Dieter pulled it from his pack anyway. The knife didn't look as shiny and new as it had on that long-ago proud day, but then, like Dieter, it had been through a lot.

Joe's eyes flickered over the blade.

"Don't kill me!" he shouted. "I won't cause no trouble. Please don't kill me!"

"I won't hurt you," Dieter said reassuringly, quickly returning the knife to his pack.

With the knife out of sight, Joe lapsed back into apathy.

As the war progressed, life in Berlin became harder. Many goods were scarce in the shops, and prices went up. Ernst failed to get a promotion, and Elsa had to be let go. It was a sad morning when she left, clutching her one battered suitcase. Elsa had been with Ernst and Eva since before the children were born. She was almost one of the family.

"Where will you go?" Dieter had asked.

"To my sister's down in Saxony. That is too far for the bombers to go. You should all get out of Berlin, too. It is not safe here anymore."

Finally, with a last hug, she had left. After that, the apartment had seemed empty, and Greta had wandered around sniffling and complaining about how much she missed Elsa. But soon her spirits rose again and Elsa was forgotten.

The bombing raids were became more frequent and heavier, and the family took to sleeping in the cellar with the other tenants. Night after night, Dieter lay listening to the distant crump of the bombs.

With Elsa gone, Eva fussed over the children — worrying about where they were going and whether they were dressed warmly enough. Ernst became even more silent and pensive. Every evening, he would closet himself in his study and listen to the BBC radio broadcasts. Only Greta appeared as cheerful as ever.

Reinhard's letters from France were read avidly.

"This is a wonderful country," he wrote in December 1942. "It's not like Russia at all. There are a few partisans who occasionally blow up a railway line, but they are not well organized. Most people are friendly and sell us food and wine. I had leave last week and spent three days in Paris. I climbed the Eiffel Tower and saw Napoleon's tomb.

"We are well rested and our numbers have been made up with new recruits, so we will be on our way back to Russia soon. I do not think I will get leave this Christmas. I hope you can manage the goose without me."

There was a goose for Christmas dinner, but it was a scrawny thing, not the plump bird of the year before. With Reinhard absent, there was no argument, but the occasion was subdued. The mood was further depressed when the radio broadcast a Christmas message from von Paulus's Sixth Army, besieged in Stalingrad. The words were brave and still spoke of ultimate victory, but they couldn't disguise the fact that the situation was desperate.

"It's like the Kaiser's war all over again," Ernst said glumly. "Two armies sitting immobile and pounding each other to a pulp. Have we learned nothing? I'm going to bed."

On February 2, 1943, the last German soldiers in Stalingrad surrendered. Three weeks later, the last Jews of Berlin were sent east.

+ + +

On February 27, 1943, Dieter was walking home alone after a soccer game with his friends. As he turned the corner, he saw a truck parked outside the Rothsteins' shop. SS soldiers in black uniforms with silver death's-head badges on their caps were throwing the Rothsteins' furniture and clothing from their flat above the shop. Dieter was embarrassed when Mrs. Rothstein's voluminous underwear drifted down to the pavement.

Dieter had barely thought about the Rothstein's for months. Five days after the night of the broken glass, Jewish children had been banned from German schools — and Dieter's secret wish not to have Marcus in his class had been granted.

The Rothsteins had struggled to keep their shop open. They had boarded up the window and carried on, but Germans were no longer allowed to buy from them. The few Jewish families in the neighborhood were too scared to go out and, in any case, had little money to spend. The other two Jewish shops on the street were taken over by Germans. Marcus disappeared, and Mr. Rothstein haunted his shop, a haggard figure in its gloomy depths. But Mrs. Rothstein stood in the shop doorway, the yellow star of David that all Jews were required to wear sewn onto her apron. She always had a kind word or a candy for Dieter and Greta as they passed.

This time, Mr. and Mrs. Rothstein appeared, disheveled and upset. They were being hustled along by Alfred, the boy who had shouted to Reinhard from the passing truck more than four years before. Alfred had been Reinhard's closest friend, and a frequent visitor to the apartment, until one day Ernst had lost his temper and angrily objected to the illogic of assigning so many resources and men to resettling the Jews when there was a war to be won. Dieter suspected

there was more to his Father's outburst than
logic. Even he'd noticed that Alfred's opinions
were uglier and more violent than Reinhard's.
And there was an unpleasant arrogance about
him — Alfred was never wrong.

After that day, Alfred had come around less
often, which was fine with Dieter. Both Reinhard
and Alfred were in the SS, but there was no way
Dieter could see his brother herding the
Rothsteins into the back of a truck. Alfred
seemed to be enjoying his work.

As Dieter stood on the sidewalk, the
Rothsteins were marched in front of him. Mr.
Rothstein looked defeated, shuffling toward the
truck as if he didn't care where it would take
him, but Mrs. Rothstein held her head high and
looked defiantly at the few passersby who had
gathered to watch. She caught Dieter's eye and
smiled. Without thinking, Dieter smiled back.
Mrs. Rothstein suddenly leaned over until her
mouth was close to Dieter's ear. "Thank your
mother," she whispered. Then she was gone,
hustled on by Alfred. Dieter looked around for
Marcus, but there was no sign of him.

The canvas canopy at the back of the truck
was pulled down and the vehicle roared off,
leaving the Rothsteins' belongings broken and
scattered on the road. Only Alfred remained, to

guard against looting before the flat could be officially cleared.

"Hey, Dieter," he yelled. "Reinhard's missing all the fun again."

"He's at the front," Dieter explained.

"Yeah?" Alfred said. "I'm heading east next month to finish the Russkies. Just helping to clean out Berlin before I go."

Dieter looked at the disappearing truck. "What'll happen to them?" he asked.

Alfred shrugged. "Who cares, as long as they're not around here? Listen, if Reinhard gets leave in the next few weeks, tell him to give me a call, okay?"

"Sure." Dieter nodded and made his way through the debris.

That evening, Dieter told his parents, "I saw the Rothsteins taken away for resettlement today. Mrs. Rothstein said I was to thank you, Mother."

Eva gasped and put her hand to her mouth. Ernst looked at his wife. He didn't say anything, but he didn't look happy.

"What did she mean?" Dieter asked.

"Nothing," said Ernst. "We were good customers, that's all. It is best to forget about the Rothsteins."

+ + +

Dieter went to meet Reinhard at the train station on Christmas Eve 1943. It was only eighteen months since Reinhard had shown up at Dieter's swearing in, but he had aged years. He was very thin and his uniform, although clean and pressed, was very worn. But it was when Dieter looked into his brother's eyes that he realized how much he had really changed. They used to sparkle with life and fun; now they were glazed, as if the things they had seen had sucked them dry. Reinhard was beginning to look like the death's-head badge on his cap.

As the pair hurried home through the gathering dusk, Dieter peppered his brother with questions about the war. There had been a lot of bad news in the past year — the defeats at Stalingrad and Kursk and the Allied landings in Italy, but there had been good news too.

"We showed them at Dieppe," Dieter enthused. "It'll be a long time before Churchill tries to land in France again."

"That was just a raid. It won't change anything." That was all Dieter could get out of his brother until they arrived at the door of their apartment block. Reinhard put his hand on

Dieter's shoulder. "Listen, Dieter, before we go up — I don't want to talk about the war in front of Mother and Greta. I know you are keen to hear stories, but please don't ask about it in the house. The war is different. It used to be glorious and triumphant, but now we are fighting just to survive. We shall still be victorious, but there will be much suffering. This war is unlike anything the world has seen. Things happen that you cannot imagine."

"Like what?" Dieter asked.

"Your turn is coming — then you will find out. I understand now what the Führer meant when he said we must make ourselves steel. There are things we must do that are hard, but we must not weaken. I have seen ..."

Reinhard drifted off. Dieter had no idea what his brother was talking about, but his seriousness was frightening. He waited for Reinhard to continue. When he did, his voice was much lighter.

"Never mind that. Let's go up and see what Mother has found for us to eat. I'm famished. Combat rations are not home cooking. But remember, no questions."

The flurry of delighted squeals and hugs at Reinhard's arrival had just died down when the air raid sirens wailed their first warning of the night.

"The first warnings are usually false," Ernst said. "We will have dinner before going to the cellar."

The family dinner was very different from that Christmas dinner only two years before. Then there had been hope, and good food. Now there was a military situation only a miracle could salvage and a meager meal. Eva had procured a small ham from somewhere, and there were potatoes and cabbage from the allotments in the Tiergarten, but it looked all the poorer set out on the shining silverware. Ernst brought out his last two bottles of good Rhine wine and everyone, including ten-year-old Greta, was given a glass.

Before the meal, Eva asked for a blessing on the house and family for the coming year. They ate rapidly and in silence, since no one knew how soon the bombers would arrive. After the meal, Ernst produced the end of a bottle of brandy and some stale cigars and proposed a toast to the German people. Reinhard replied with one to Adolf Hitler.

"Hitler," Ernst said scornfully. "That damned man has brought ruin on Germany."

There was a shocked silence. Even in private, Germans were loath to speak out so openly.

"Damn it," Ernst went on, "it needs saying, and if I cannot speak my mind in my own dining room, I might as well be dead. I thought it was bad after the First War, but I fear that will be nothing compared to what it will be like when the Russians get here."

"We'll stop the Russians," Reinhard said uncomfortably.

"With what?" Ernst challenged. "Shall we throw potatoes at them? We have lots of those, but not much else."

Reinhard perked up. "Our new Tiger tanks are better than anything the Russians have."

"Is that why we lost at Kursk?" Ernst asked derisively.

"We lost at Kursk because our plans were betrayed," Reinhard said. "Some Jew got hold of them and sold them to the Russians. They were waiting for us."

"The Jews, the Jews," Ernst said. "It's always the Jews. Never our fault. The Führer can't make mistakes. It must be the Jewish Conspiracy. And where are all those conspiratorial Jews anyway? I haven't seen one in the streets for ages." Ernst sounded bitter and angry. His taunting tone was going to cause an explosion even worse than the one two years ago.

Dieter turned to Reinhard for his answer, but his brother just stared at his brandy.

Encouraged, Ernst continued. "I'll tell you where they are, resettled, just like you said they would be. I've seen the trains leaving for the east. They pack those poor people in like sardines. Whole families — old, young — I've seen babies in their mother's arms. It's barbaric. They lose their homes, their jobs, their possessions — and for what? Some barren piece of land in the conquered territories?"

"Ernst —" Eva attempted to interrupt, but Ernst cut her off.

"No, Eva, it needs to be said. You have looked positively on things, believing they would get no worse. I have always said that no good would come of having a brute like Hitler in charge. But I have been wrong, too — things are much worse than even I suspected, and now we have no choice but to stay here and endure — if we can. All I can do is try to force some sense into my son. Reinhard does not seem to understand the human misery caused by the policies he and his party of thugs espouse. They have ruined this country and dragged us into a war we cannot win. All because of some half-baked nonsense about being a master race. I am ashamed of my son for the part he has played in this; but more, I am ashamed of myself and all other decent Germans who allowed it to happen."

Ernst sat back, exhausted by his diatribe. Still Reinhard sat silent with his head bowed. His cigar had gone out.

Dieter felt he had to protect his brother from the attack. "The Jews are happy in the east. We were shown movies at school. They have model communities. Everyone was smiling and busy. Families played in the parks. They weren't being bombed every night. It looked much better than here. I wouldn't mind being resettled."

"Never ever say that!" Reinhard shouted, his eyes blazing. Dieter looked at him in shock.

"Don't ever say you want to be treated like a Jew," Reinhard went on. "They are subhuman. The Führer understands that we must have a final solution to the Jewish problem. We must steel ourselves to the task. You civilians can never understand."

Reinhard turned to Ernst. "What would you have me do? The past cannot be changed, however much you whip yourself for your inaction. Our enemies will not stop until we are crushed, our cities piles of rubble — or until we prevail. I am fighting for Germany now, not some ideal. I have no choice, and neither do you or … anyone."

Reinhard's voice trailed off and the fire left his eyes. His blank look returned, and he idly turned the cigar between his fingers. Was

Reinhard going mad? Dieter hurriedly pushed the thought away. It was exhaustion, that's all.

Greta eventually broke the silence. "Mrs. Rothstein wasn't subhuman. She used to give us candy. Where is she?"

Reinhard squeezed his eyes shut to hold back tears. "Smoke," he murmured.

"What was that?" Ernst asked.

Reinhard made a visible effort to regain his self-control. "Nothing, Father," he said, wiping his eyes. "Listen, no matter what we think of one another, we must not fight. We are a family, and whatever else happens, we will always have that."

"You are right," Ernst said.

Reinhard nodded. "Anyway, I have some news. I am being transferred to a new unit, the Twelfth SS Panzer Division — the Hitlerjugend, of Hitler Youth members. Some junior officers have been moved from the Leibstandarte to train the boys."

"Yes," Dieter interrupted excitedly, "they have been asking the older boys to volunteer at our meetings."

"That's the other piece of news," Reinhard said. "Word is that the Führer is going to reduce the age of conscription to sixteen."

Eva gasped and clutched her napkin to her mouth.

"That's ridiculous," Ernst spluttered. "They can't use boys in war."

"They can, Father," Reinhard said, "and they will. Probably by Dieter's next birthday he will be old enough."

"I won't let him go," Eva said in a shaky voice. "I'll hide him."

"He'll be found. Everyone is registered. If Dieter doesn't go when he is called, they will come and get him. You and Father would be jailed."

"No," Eva said weakly. "Please, Reinhard."

"He's right," Ernst agreed. "Dieter will have to go."

"Look, if you do nothing, Dieter will be conscripted in a few months. He will be assigned to any old unit and be sent to God knows where. If he goes now and requests a place in the Hitlerjugend, he will go sooner, but I can arrange it so he is put in my unit," Reinhard suggested. "That way, I can keep an eye on him."

The thoughtful silence around the table was broken only by Eva's quiet sobs. Reinhard's strange behavior bothered Dieter, and the war was not going well. The cinema newsreels rarely showed German troops triumphantly entering a captured town, as they had in the war's early days. Even Ernst had stopped listening to the BBC — it was too depressing. Dieter wanted to go to the war — but so soon?

"I think that is what we should do," Ernst said. "It will mean Dieter goes off a bit earlier than —"

"But it's so dangerous," Eva said. "He's just a boy!"

"Yes," Ernst agreed, "but it is dangerous here, too, and who knows how bad the bombing is going to get before this is all over. Reinhard's idea is a good one."

Dieter gazed at the flickering lights to the north where the bombing raid was ending, then back at his companion. Joe was slumped to one side. Dieter switched on his flashlight. Joe's eyes were closed and his jaw hung slack and open.

"Joe!" Dieter said, shaking his shoulder. He got no response. A wave of panic overwhelmed Dieter. This one limp figure was his only hope. He mustn't die!

"Joe!" Dieter repeated, shaking more vigorously. "Don't die. I need you. Listen!"

To Dieter's relief, Joe opened his eyes. "So tired," he mumbled. Dieter propped Joe's head up and gave him a sip of water. That helped, but Dieter had to get Joe to focus.

"I was telling you how I came to join the army," he said. "Why did you join up? Why fight in a war on the other side of the world?"

"Join up?" Joe asked in a confused voice.

"Yes," Dieter encouraged. "Why are you fighting Germans in Europe instead of making buttons in Canada?"

"Spain," Joe said after a moment's intense thought.

"What?"

"Spain," Joe repeated. Then slowly, with many interruptions and much encouragement from Dieter, the story came out. "My Uncle Norm, he went to Spain in nineteen thirty-seven. Reckoned no one was doing enough to fight against Fascism, so he went to fight for the Republic against Franco. He lost, of course. Came back a bitter man. Said it was the government's fault he had lost. Mussolini sent thousands of soldiers, tanks and guns. Hitler sent a whole air force. What did Canada and the others do? Nothing. Even tried to stop men going as volunteers. Just sat back and let the Fascists roll over the people.

"Norm said it wasn't surprising since most of the high-ups in government were almost Fascist themselves. Even the prime minister, Mackenzie King, admired Hitler — said he had nice eyes. I wonder if all them dead Jews thought so, too?

"Anyway, Norm was always going on about how we had to stop Fascism, else we'd all end up in concentration camps. When the war broke out, he was one of the first to join up. Me and Tom weren't far behind. There was no work at home anyways, and it felt good to think you were doing something to help.

"Not that we did much — just sat around and trained for the longest time. We thought Norm was the lucky one. He joined the South Saskatchewans. They were one of the first outfits into action. But poor old Norm got blown to bits on the beach at Dieppe. Hope he managed to take a few Nazis with him. That would have made him happy.

"Me and Tom was luckier, spending all our pay on weak English beer and our leave chasing plump English girls. Good days … I guess Tom's luck ran out when we met that Tiger. But we got it, too, brewed it up good. Norm would have liked that."

Joe's story was so strange, so opposite from what Dieter had been told. All the things he admired most were thought evil. It had all seemed so simple once: all you had to do was believe the good things Hitler said and everything would be fine. But instead, everything had fallen apart.

Suddenly, Joe's pale face in the flashlight's beam was Reinhard. The same high cheekbones, long face and fair hair. Dieter tried to shake the idea out of his head, but couldn't. If Ernst had had his way — if they had gone to Canada back when they were children — how would Reinhard have turned out? Like Joe? Perhaps Reinhard would have joined the Canadian army. Maybe he would have ended up dead on a beach like Norm or with his chest blown open like Tom.

Perhaps it made no difference what you did.

Dieter sighed, switched off the flashlight and continued with his story. "I joined the Hitlerjugend just after New Year's 1944. Reinhard fixed it so that I could join his unit. They were stationed in France. The training was hard, but, like you in England, we had time for fun, too. Like Reinhard had said in his letters, most of the French seemed happy to live and let live. Then you landed at Normandy. We were sent to meet you."

The twenty-three survivors of Reinhard's battle group huddled in the abbey cellar as the heavy shells from the battleships offshore pounded into the ruins above their heads. The air was filled with choking brick dust, the walls spat fragments of stone with each explosion and the ground shook as if the earth itself were trying to throw these annoying humans off its back. The concussions were like hammers thundering down on each man's brain. This had been going on for hours, and the urge to get up and run, anywhere, was almost overwhelming. But outside the cellar there was only death.

"Stay where you are!" Reinhard screamed as he saw men steal glances at the cellar steps. "Our only chance is to stay here. Find something to hold on to. Hug it as if it were your mother. And it is. Whatever you hold onto in here that stops you running outside will give you life as surely as your mother did. Don't think — just focus on holding on."

Dieter had long ago ceased to think. He didn't even feel scared anymore. His conscious mind had given up trying to compete with the barrage.

All he was aware of was the ancient pillar he was trying to crush in his embrace and the pain that shot through his hip every time the pillar vibrated from a nearby shell. Vaguely, somewhere at the back of his mind, Dieter knew that as soon as the shelling stopped, the Canadians would attack again, but he almost welcomed that. Anything, if only this noise would stop.

Beside Dieter, Karl had his eyes closed and was quietly singing. As the noise waxed and waned, Dieter caught fragments of song, but mostly he knew his friend was singing because his lips were moving. Karl had begun with the Horst Wessel song and other Nazi anthems, but now he was reduced to children's songs and Christmas carols.

Dieter loved carols. They conjured up an image of his family sitting happily by the fire, Father with his deep voice and Greta with her thin, squeaky baby voice. Even Reinhard had —

Why was Reinhard shouting at him and shaking his shoulder? What was he saying?

"They're coming. We have to go."

Gradually, a silence enveloped Dieter. It meant something. What? The shelling had stopped. The Canadians were coming again. Regretfully releasing the pillar, Dieter grabbed his rifle and headed up the steps.

Even through clouds of smoke and dust, the sunlight hurt Dieter's eyes. Squinting painfully, he stumbled across what had been the abbey courtyard and flung himself on a pile of rubble. Karl landed beside him and got busy aligning the group's only machine gun down the destroyed street in front of them. Behind them, Reinhard directed others into the buildings on either side to better cover the length of the street and to keep them from being flanked.

Dieter peered out over the wasteland. The street was almost clogged with collapsed walls, and flames licked hungrily from windows of shattered buildings. Dieter's eye drifted up to the second floor of a building on his right. It had been an apartment before the entire front wall had been blown into the street. Now everything inside was exposed, just like Greta's dollhouse. Curtains still hung in the back windows, a painting of a pastoral landscape stood out against flower-patterned wallpaper. A grand piano balanced precariously from one ruined floor. The keyboard was open and the lid propped up. Instead of a pianist, the stool was occupied by a black enamel sewing machine. The scene reminded Dieter of the surrealist pictures in the degenerate art catalog that Reinhard had shown him so long ago.

He was about to point this out to Karl when he caught a movement out of the corner of his eye. Dieter squinted hard at a dark patch at the far end of the street. He had just about convinced himself that it was nothing when the patch detached itself from the wall, became a man and launched into a stumbling run diagonally down the street.

"There!" Dieter shouted, but Karl had seen the figure, too. The machine gun stuttered a short burst and the distant figure flopped to the ground like a rag doll.

"Got him!" Karl yelled triumphantly, an instant before bullets sprayed along the street toward them.

"Keep your heads down. Hold your fire until they show themselves!" Reinhard shouted. That was difficult, being shot at and not shooting back but, like many things Reinhard had learned in Russia, it made sense — you didn't give away your position or strength; and, you didn't waste always scarce ammunition.

Dieter hunkered low and let the bullets fly over his head. He smiled ruefully. So this was his dream come true. Here he was in uniform, but not one of the elegant ones he remembered from the parades before the war. Dieter's uniform was baggy, mottled camouflage combat fatigues criss-crossed with belts carrying everything from ammunition to a water bottle. Even his helmet was smeared with dirt to make it less visible. It didn't look pretty, but it was efficient.

Dieter had been in battle amid the ruins of Caen for a month, a hardened soldier. Reinhard had extraordinary expertise, which he struggled to pass on to his teenage soldiers. Despite Reinhard's teaching, many had been killed. The battle group that had gone into Caen on the day after the Allied invasion was down to half strength. Soon that half would be gone, too. There were no reserves to relieve them, and their orders were to hold on to the last bullet.

Even ordinary soldiers like Dieter had heard that the Hitlerjugend commander, Kurt Meyer, had railed against that order. He knew it was futile, but the order had come direct from the Führer, so hold on they would, although the overwhelming numbers of Canadian soldiers and tanks left the final outcome in no doubt. Dieter was vaguely wondering if any of the men coming toward him had fathers who'd fought against his father in the Kaiser's war, when Karl's machine gun opened up beside him with a loud stutter.

"Here they come!" Reinhard shouted.

Dieter pushed himself up the rubble pile and peered down the street. Damn it, they had a tank. The sloping front of the Sherman rose and fell as it rumbled over the rubble. Behind it, shapes darted along the walls, firing occasionally. The machine gun on the tank stuttered a reply to Karl. Dieter watched a figure slip into a doorway. Patiently, he aimed at the dark space. The figure stepped out. Dieter squeezed the trigger. The figure jerked backward and fell. Smoothly, Dieter worked the bolt of his rifle. The Sherman fired, and an explosion to Dieter's right showered him with fragments. He was vaguely aware of someone screaming.

Dieter fired again, not a carefully aimed shot this time. The tank was closer, its barrel pointing straight at them. It was going for Karl's machine gun.

The exploding shell hurled Dieter backward and ripped the rifle out of his hands. Dieter's ears hurt, and he couldn't hear anything. In slow motion, he looked around. The top half of Karl's body lay beside him. There was no sign of his legs. His friend's eyes blinked in surprise. Beneath him, Dieter felt the ground vibrate, but still heard nothing. Then the treads of the Sherman loomed over the pile of rubble, churning the stones into tiny avalanches.

I'm going to be crushed, Dieter thought disinterestedly. Then Reinhard was there, his face close to Dieter's. He was saying something, shouting by the look of it, but still Dieter couldn't hear. Reinhard was tugging at his arm now. How annoying big brothers could be! All Dieter wanted to do was lie back and see what it was like to be crushed. But Reinhard looked frantic. It must be important — perhaps Dieter's mother wanted him. He supposed he should go. With a sigh, Dieter rolled over and scrambled after his brother. Behind him, the tank crashed down the rubble slope.

Dieter followed Reinhard through a hole in a wall, across a room with only two walls and no roof, and along a narrow alley. Eventually, Reinhard ducked into a doorway. Dieter followed him and found himself in another dark cellar — he seemed to live most of his life in these places. Reinhard slumped against a wall and took out his water bottle.

"That was close," he said, offering the bottle to Dieter. Dieter accepted it and took a long drink.

"Hold on," Reinhard said, taking the bottle back. "Take small sips. That way, the water lasts longer."

Dieter's ears still hurt, but he was glad he could hear again.

"Thanks," he said as he remembered Reinhard dragging him away from the tank. "Where are the others?"

Reinhard shrugged. "Dead or captured, I suppose," he said bitterly. "How do they expect us to fight? We don't have tanks or anti-tank guns. There are no reserves, and supplies hardly ever get through the bombardment." He spat disgustedly into the dust. "Some of those secret weapons Goebbels is always talking about had better show up quickly."

"Can we still win?" Dieter asked.

"Of course we can," Reinhard responded, but his voice lacked conviction. "Anyway, we have no choice but to keep fighting."

"We could surrender. We don't all have to die."

Reinhard let out a sharp laugh. "Surrender," he said. "Perhaps some can do that, but not us."

"Why not?" Dieter asked.

"Look, Brother," Reinhard said patiently, "you have turned into a good soldier. I am proud of you, I really am, but you're still a naive kid. You don't really know anything. This is not the east."

"What do you mean? The fighting couldn't be any harder than this."

"I'm not talking about the fighting."

"What then?" Dieter asked in obvious frustration.

Reinhard looked hard at his brother. "There are things …" he began. "No. It is best you do not know. Just know that the SS has done things the enemy will not easily forgive. After this is over, they will hunt down all of us with tattoos on our left arms."

"I don't have one," Dieter said.

"What?"

"I don't have a tattoo." Dieter elaborated. "There wasn't time after I joined up. They rushed us out here for training, and then the landings happened. They said we would get one after we had thrown the British back into the sea."

Reinhard laughed. "I always said you were the lucky one in the family. Well, don't let them give you one." Reinhard absentmindedly fingered his left arm. "You might escape yet."

"But what 'things' has the SS done?" Dieter insisted.

Reinhard was prevented from replying by a shell exploding in the alley outside and a figure crashing through the doorway in a cloud of dust.

"Well, hello, Alfred," Reinhard said, getting to his feet. "I suppose this means that we should be moving along. Come on, Little Brother. We have to stay alive a bit longer in this hell hole."

"Hell hole is right." Joe was more animated than Dieter had seen him all night.

"What?" Dieter asked, confused at being wrenched from his memories.

"Caen," Joe said. "It sure was a hell hole."

"You were there?"

"'Course we were. Me and Tom and the whole Third Division went through it all, the shelling, the bombing, the fighting for every room. God only knows what would have happened if the Jerries had managed to get their tanks through. Got to thank the air force for that one. Blew them Panzers to bits before they got to Caen. Don't reckon we could have taken the town if they hadn't."

Joe had been at Caen! Had he and Dieter shot at each other? Strange. Now here they were, sitting in a field near a burning tank swapping stories.

"And those SS kids were the worst," Joe went on. "Fanatics. Never gave up until they were dead — boys of fifteen or sixteen throwing themselves through machine-gun fire to stuff a grenade into the tracks of a Sherman. It was suicide, plain and simple, but it scared the hell out of us. Never knew which cellar had a crazy kid ready to die for his Führer in it.

"Once, we found the bodies of two of our boys. Shot in the head — executed after they had surrendered. Made the captain real mad. He said we were not to take any prisoners for the next week. Some men took it to heart and never sent any prisoners back, but I couldn't. They were just kids, after all. Crazy, dangerous kids, but kids.

"Almost killed me, that mistake. Captured one of the little rats and was taking him back when he went for me with that small knife they all carry. Slashed my arm, but Tom put a bullet in him before he could do too much damage."

So that was why Joe had flinched at the sight of Dieter's knife. Dieter was immensely relieved that Joe, in his dazed state, had not made the connection between the knife Dieter had shown him and the SS he had fought at Caen. As Joe talked, Dieter slipped the knife from his pack and pressed it into the long grass by his side. That was another piece of his past hidden.

"Hey, Tom! We saved each other's life a dozen times, didn't we?" Joe began sobbing. "But I couldn't save you from that damned Tiger."

Dieter couldn't let Joe lapse into self-pity and give up. He had to keep him focused on the fight to survive.

"After Caen it was all retreat," Dieter said. "I got injured before Christmas 1944. I was sent home and so I missed the Ardennes offensive. At first, I was sorry not to be with Reinhard — it seemed like the old days, with the tanks rolling forward — but there were too few of them and there was no air cover. As soon as the weather cleared, the tank-killers were at it again, destroying the tanks before they could even get into battle.

"I spent Christmas in Berlin — or what was left of it."

D ieter kept slipping on the piles of rubble. A rough, winding path had been partially cleared down the middle of the street, but it was still precarious picking a way along, especially with one arm in a sling and a bag of potatoes swinging from the other. All around Dieter, the fronts of ruined buildings stood like stage sets with nothing behind them. Dark, empty window frames stared, abandoned cars sat where they had been left months before, when they ran out of gas.

It was odd, Dieter thought. The longer the war went on, the farther back in time they went. All that separated modern man from his ancestors huddling terrified in a cave was gradually being stripped away. The lights that made the city safe at night were the first to go. The vehicles that made it easy to get from one place to another were useless because the streets were impassable. Now the shops were empty. Everyone was moving back to being hunter-gatherers, scrounging for scraps and bargaining for a meal. And Greta was the best scrounger of them all.

Greta struggled along beside Dieter. Her clothes were filthy and heavily patched. Ingrid, her prized possession, much the worse for wear, was tucked into the belt of her grubby dress. Greta's only other possession, her flute, was tucked under one arm. A loaf of dark bread was under the other. With her almost uncanny knack for finding food, Greta had led Dieter to a dark cellar, where she had bargained hard for the potatoes and bread that would be their Christmas dinner. It had cost several pieces of family silver, but as Greta had gleefully told him afterward, not as much as she had thought. The remaining pieces were stuffed in a pack on Greta's back, making her look like an old hunchbacked woman from a medieval painting. Dieter smiled.

"What are you grinning at?" Greta asked. "Do you want to carry the pack?"

"No, no," Dieter replied. "I was just thinking how well you have adapted to this life."

"What's to adapt to? We're hungry. We need food. We have something that we cannot eat. Someone will give us food for it. So we exchange. It's simple."

"I know. It's simple when you say it, but not everyone finds it as easy as you do."

Greta shrugged.

Dieter was very proud of his sister. With the extraordinary resilience of an eleven-year-old, she had thrived in this life among the ruins. Perhaps for her, war was the normal way of the world. But Greta had also adapted — perhaps too well — to the horrors around her. Just a couple of days before, they had come upon a body when they were clambering through a ruined building. Dieter had seen many bodies, but they still unsettled him, especially civilians. This one had been an old man — he must have been caught outside when a bomb exploded nearby. It had destroyed most of his body; there was not much left except his head and legs. Instinctively, Dieter had turned to shield Greta from the scene, but she had pushed past him, unconcerned by the disgusting sight and sickly smell.

"Those shoes must be about Father's size," she had said, untying the laces.

"Greta!" Dieter had been horrified at his sister's callousness. "You can't."

"Why not?" she'd replied. "He doesn't need them anymore and Father is almost barefoot."

Her logic was impeccable, but the sight of his sister casually taking the shoes off a mutilated corpse had made Dieter queasy.

Dieter had been home for three weeks. Considering the danger he had survived in the past year, it was almost funny how he had broken his arm. He'd been walking back from guard duty when he slipped on a patch of ice. He had thrown out his left arm to stop himself and landed heavily on his elbow. He'd heard the loud snap of the break before he even felt any pain.

Dieter's arm was healing, but slowly because of the lack of food. His mother kept pushing what meager supplies the family had at him, saying he had to eat to regain his strength, but Dieter refused as much as he could. His mother needed the food more than he did. She was the weakest, and Dieter suspected she was giving part of her food to Greta and his father. Eva was like a skeleton. Her sunken eyes above her gaunt cheekbones flitted about the almost-bare apartment. She seemed obsessed with keeping the rooms clean, an impossible task given the bomb dust that covered everything after each nightly raid. Dieter had tried to talk her out of it, but she had refused, saying over and over that it was her job to keep the house tidy.

Once, Dieter had found her sitting on the floor in the parlor hugging her knees and weeping.

"What's the matter?"

"I was wrong," Eva replied, looking at her son through her tears. "Ernst was right. We should have gone to Canada. We would be safe now. I was scared to leave everything I knew and loved. I never thought things would get this bad. It's my fault we are in this mess."

"Don't say that!" Dieter cried. "It's not your fault. Anyway, we'll manage. As long as we stick together and help one another."

Eva smiled weakly at Dieter. "You're a good boy," she said. Then, more seriously, "If anything happens — if we are ... split up — I want you and Greta to go to Uncle Walter's farm. Things will be better in the country. Walter will look after you. Ernst doesn't care much for him, but he is a good man. Promise me?"

"Nothing's going to happen, Mother."

"Promise me."

"I promise. If we have to leave the city, I will take Greta and go to Uncle Walter."

Eva relaxed. "Good. I have written out directions for you." She pulled a scrap of paper from her apron pocket and handed it to Dieter. "His farm is on the road to Wittenberge, not far from Neustadt. It's all written there. You promise, now?"

"Yes, Mother, I promise."

Eva nodded her satisfaction. Then her eyes drifted off and she began rocking slowly. "Look at that mantel," she said distractedly. "It needs a good dusting."

Ernst, too, was thin and pale, but he conserved more of his strength. He sat in the one remaining armchair, silently gazing out the window over the Tiergarten or at the fire when they found something to burn.

Greta was skinny and her sparkling eyes were surrounded by dark shadows, but somehow she maintained good cheer.

"I think you broke your arm just so you wouldn't have to carry the pack."

"That's right," Dieter replied. "In fact, the whole war is just so that I don't have to carry the pack. I talked to Hitler in 1939 and persuaded him to invade Poland just so the war would be well under way when I was old enough to join up. That way, I could break my arm so that my little sister had to carry the family silver to exchange for potatoes for Christmas dinner."

Greta laughed, a beautiful tinkling, glasslike sound, so fragile and joyful amid all the black desolation of the bombed city. Dieter found himself going out of his way to provoke it, just because it made him feel so happy.

"Well," Greta replied, "I'm carrying the silver now, so Hitler can tell everyone to stop fighting." She laughed again, but this time it sounded hollow. "Do you think the war will be over soon?"

"Yes," Dieter replied honestly. "I think the war will be over very soon."

"And we won't win, will we?"

"No, we won't."

"What will happen when we lose?"

It was a question that had been much on Dieter's mind lately. Before he broke his arm, some of his comrades had talked about not fighting in the west so that the Americans could invade Germany and stop the Russians. The optimists even talked of the Americans joining the Germans to fight the Communists, but that was wishful thinking. The Americans might fight the Russians, but Germany would be crushed first. Dieter could only hope that the Americans got to Berlin before the Russians. Everyone had heard the stories about what the Russian soldiers did to the towns they captured. Maybe it would make no difference. Whoever arrived first would hunt down the SS.

"I don't know," he said weakly. "Look, there's the Rothsteins' store. We're almost home." Although a German family had taken over the business, Dieter's family still referred to it by its old name. The store was still open, but no one bought material anymore.

It was easier to walk now — the bombing had been less heavy here. A woman passed them pushing a pram with a mattress precariously balanced on top, her eyes fixed on it.

"Carry the bread and I'll play you a tune," Greta offered.

"Okay," Dieter replied, stuffing the loaf in his sling. Greta lifted her flute to one side and licked her lips. The first delicate notes drifted out along the street and through the broken apartment windows.

Dieter loved his sister's flute playing even more than her laugh. She practiced constantly — sometimes to the annoyance of their mother and father — and had become quite good. She had a wide repertoire, from slow, serious, formal pieces to light, happy dances. Mostly, these days, she played the dances, which was fine with Dieter. He needed music, Greta's and any other music he heard, to help him forget his troubles. Through the magic of Greta's notes, Dieter could feel his mood improving. He understood how the Pied Piper of Hamelin could have led the rats and the children off to the hills.

Greta kept playing as they entered their apartment block and climbed the dusty stairs. Eva met them at the door. "Are you all right?" she fussed. "You were so long."

"We're fine," Greta said, lowering her flute. Dieter handed over the potatoes and the bread. The muscles in his arm tingled with relief. Eva hurried down the corridor to the kitchen.

As Dieter flexed his stiff arm, he became aware of a rasping sound from the dining room. With a puzzled frown, he went to investigate. Greta followed. The sight that met him made him stop so suddenly that Greta cannoned into his back. In the middle of the room, their beautiful dining table lay on its side. Ernst was crouched, like a feasting vulture, industriously sawing away at one of the legs. He had already cut off the foot, but the wood was thicker where it joined the tabletop.

"What are you doing, Father?" Dieter asked, horrified at the desecration of his favorite piece of furniture.

"Getting firewood," Ernst replied through his heavy breathing. He put down the saw, picked up a hammer and began hitting the partly cut leg.

"Damn it," he swore quietly each time his ineffectual blow bounced off the hard wood. He was obviously nearly exhausted.

"But that's our table," Dieter said pointlessly.

"Of course, it is," Greta said, pushing past him and handing him her flute. "And it's no use now. We don't need a beautiful table to eat soggy cabbage and sprouting potatoes. "Give me that." Greta took the hammer from her father. Holding it in both hands, she hauled it back as far as she could and swung it against the leg with all her might. With a deafening crack, the leg fell.

"There," she said triumphantly, "that should burn nicely." Dropping the hammer, she picked up the ends of the two pieces of leg and dragged them to the parlor. Her father and brother followed.

Ernst settled himself in his chair and recovered his breath. Greta busied herself by the grate. A small fire was already burning fitfully. Tearing pages out of a book lying nearby, Greta gradually built up the fire. When it was a respectable size, she placed the smaller piece of table leg over it. The wood was too long for the grate but it fitted in at an angle. Soon the flames were licking around the wood and the gleaming varnish was bubbling. Greta wiped her hands on her dress, sat back and took her flute from Dieter.

Dieter could feel the heat on his legs. Only then did he realize how cold he was after their excursion. He huddled beside Greta, who lifted her flute and began playing a cheerful folk song.

"Don't block all the heat," Ernst grumbled behind them. The children moved back. "And stop that damned racket. It's worse than an air raid."

"I can play if I want to," Greta said defensively.

"Not if I can hear you," Ernst replied.

"Fine. If you don't like it, you don't have to listen. I'll play it in my room." Greta stomped out.

Dieter was amazed. One minute Greta could be the most practical person in the family, scrounging food or demolishing a table for firewood; the next, she was a little girl, storming off in a snit.

"That wasn't fair," he said to his father.

"It's not a fair world," Ernst replied, reaching for his pipe. There had been no tobacco for months, and Ernst had tried smoking all manner of things, from tea leaves to garden weeds dried in the oven, but nothing had worked. Now he just took what comfort he could from fiddling with the empty bowl.

"But I wish Reinhard could be with us," Ernst said. "The boy's always been a hotheaded fool, but families should be together at Christmas. God knows if any of us will see next Christmas."

"Of course we will," Dieter replied automatically. "The war will be over and everything will be fine again."

"I am afraid that very little will ever be fine again. The Americans and the British have eight armies just waiting for the weather to improve before they cross the Rhine. It is said that, to the east, the Russians have three million men even closer. As soon as spring comes, they will attack. Then it will all be over.

"And the victors will not be forgiving. That madman has led us to destruction and caused untold suffering and devastation. We must all take some of the blame. Some people, like Reinhard, eagerly embraced the new order. Others, like your mother and me, merely did nothing, hoping that things would work out. Who is to say who carries more guilt? In any case, I suspect it is not a distinction the Russians will make. As always in war, the innocent will suffer with the guilty.

"So, I want to give you some advice. It may not be much use, but it is all I have left to give."

"Father, don't be so —" Dieter began, but Ernst stopped him.

"No," he said. "Hear me out. You may do what I suggest or not, but do me the courtesy of listening without interruption." Dieter nodded silently. "Do you remember I told you about Allen Shardlow, the Canadian who captured me in the last war?"

"Yes," Dieter replied. "It was my favorite story."

"Good. I once dreamed of our family starting a new life in Canada. We didn't. I don't blame Eva. What's done is done. Perhaps I should have insisted. I sometimes wonder how Reinhard would have turned out if we had gone." Ernst gazed wistfully at the fire.

"It's too late for me," he went on, "but perhaps not for you children. So I want you to promise me something. When the end comes, and it won't be long, take Greta — and Reinhard if you can find him and if he will go — and head west. If possible, find the Canadian army and surrender to them." Ernst handed Dieter a crumpled piece of paper.

"This is Allen Shardlow's address. I have not heard from him for years. He may have moved or he may be dead, but if he is alive and if you can find him, he will help you start a new life in Canada. There is nothing left in Europe but ruins and hatred. I want you children to make your futures elsewhere. Get Allen's help if you can, but go to Canada in any case."

"We will all go," Dieter insisted.

"Maybe, but nothing is certain. I want your word that, should something happen to your mother and me, you will do whatever it takes to get at least yourself and Greta to Canada."

"Mother says we should go to Uncle Walter's farm if anything happens."

Ernst grunted. "Not such a bad idea. Walter and I have never seen eye to eye on many things, but he will not refuse to help. But it must be only a stopping place on the way to Canada. Promise me."

"Yes, Father," Dieter said, "I promise."

"So that is why I want to go to Canada," Dieter said.

Joe didn't answer. He was asleep, his chest rising and falling regularly. Dieter decided to let him be. He also kept talking. He had come so far with his tale, it was too late to stop now. Telling it aloud marked a fault line, a break between the life that was ending and the one he hoped was about to open before him.

Christmas Eve dinner was potatoes, cabbage, some coarse sausage that Greta had magically found and stale bread, served on the last of the fine silver and accompanied by harsh red wine. The family sat on packing cases in the parlor warmed by the dining room table legs burning in the grate.

In the new year, Dieter and Greta went out nearly every day to scrounge for food. Dieter's arm continued to be slow to heal. By February, Dieter could hear the Russian guns to the east. In March, despite his weak arm, he was called out with children and old people to dig anti-tank ditches around the city. By April, the bombing was so bad that the family was forced to move permanently to their apartment block's crowded cellar. By April 21, the Russians were fighting in the city suburbs. That morning, the radio announced that, in honor of Hitler's birthday the day before, the valiant civilian defenders of Fortress Berlin were to be given extra rations — half a kilogram of bacon, a quarter kilogram of rice, 250 lentils or peas, one can of vegetables, a kilogram of sugar, a little coffee and some fat. This was to last a family for eight days. Dieter and Greta hurried out into the clear, sunny morning to pick up the bounty.

"So the Führer has a birthday and we all get presents," Greta chattered happily as they picked their way through the ruined streets. "Good old Grofaz."

"Don't call him that," Dieter said, looking around to see if anyone had heard. "You'll get in trouble."

"Oh, don't be such a worrier. Everyone calls him Grofaz. It's short for Grösste Feldherr aller Zeiten; how can it be disrespectful to call him the Greatest Commander of all Time?"

"It's sarcastic. You know that."

Dieter's words had no effect. Dancing ahead of him, Greta shouted, "Don't worry. Old Grofaz will save us!"

"Be quiet!" Dieter implored. As they passed a group of old men piling cobblestones around an overturned tram to form a barricade across the boulevard, Greta calmed down and fell in step with her brother.

"I heard a joke," she announced gleefully. "How long will it take the Russians to break through?" Without waiting, she answered, "Two hours and five minutes. Two hours of laughing at our defences and five minutes to smash through them."

"It's not funny," Dieter said over Greta's laughter.

"I think it is," Greta said. "You're no fun anymore. Listen, they're showing *The Big Number* at the movie theater along Charlottenburger. It's a circus movie. I want to see it. Let's go tonight?"

"How can you talk about going to the movies?" Dieter asked harshly. "Mother is getting weaker by the day, and Father seems to have lost interest in everything. Reinhard is missing, and the Russian barbarians are at the edge of the city. And all you can do is tell jokes and think about movies."

"Well," Greta shot back angrily, "does your moaning about everything make it any better? Does an extra loaf of bread appear every time you complain? We might as well be cheerful."

Dieter sighed. Greta was impossible.

As they rounded a corner, they realized they had not been the only people listening to the radio that morning. An immense line snaked along the street and into the ration depot.

"We'll be here all day," Dieter said as they joined the line.

"It'll be worth it for some bacon," Greta replied. "I hope we get peas. I hate lentils."

Dieter glanced at his watch — 11:30. He'd hoped to be home by lunchtime, but they would be lucky to get back for dinner. The line shuffled forward a step and stopped.

"We might as well have some entertainment," Greta said, taking out her flute. As she played, people all along the street turned to listen to the delicate sound. Faces broke into smiles as people forgot their troubles for a moment.

Suddenly, Dieter lunged and grabbed the flute out of Greta's hands.

"What —" Greta began.

"Shut up!" Dieter ordered.

It was a deep, rough noise, not like the whistle of a falling bomb. Smiles were replaced by frowns of puzzlement. In a city of strange sounds, people had never heard this one — but Dieter had. In Caen.

"Artillery!" he screamed. Dropping the flute and grabbing Greta's arm, he hauled her into the nearest doorway. The noise was almost a scream now, and some people were running along the street. Most, however, stayed where they were, unwilling to give up their place in line.

The first shell exploded with a thunderous roar, hurling fragments of paving and bodies in all directions. As the line broke and people scattered, shells fell in the street and in the buildings along it. Greta cowered in the corner of the deep doorway, Dieter huddled protectively over her.

Gradually the shelling moved away, and Dieter risked a look into the rubble-strewn street. Bodies lay everywhere. Occasionally, one would move or groan. Directly in front of them lay the twisted body of a young girl in a pool of blood.

"Oh no!" Greta moaned.

Instinctively, Dieter moved between his sister and the torn corpse, but Greta pushed him out of the way.

"There's nothing you can do," Dieter said.

But Greta merely stepped over the dead girl and knelt by her flute, lying where Dieter had dropped it. A chunk of masonry had crushed the tube.

With exquisite tenderness, Greta removed the rock and cradled the wrecked instrument like a baby. Tears cut lines through the dust on her cheeks.

Dieter shook his head in confusion. Mutilated bodies had no effect on Greta, but a broken flute reduced her to a quivering wreck.

"Come on," he said. "We have to get home."

Greta made no protest as Dieter helped her to her feet, and she meekly followed a step behind him through the carnage. It wasn't until they reached their apartment block's cellar that Dieter noticed that, somewhere on the journey, Greta had dropped the flute.

The family's apartment still stood, but all the windows had been blown out and there was a gaping hole in the parlor wall. Over the past few weeks, the cellar had been transformed from an overnight shelter from the bombing to a full-time residence for most of the block's inhabitants. Because they had clung on to day-time life in their apartment as long as possible, Dieter and Greta had only been able to stake out a small space at the back of the crowded cellar for the family. It was just large enough for all of them to lie down and sleep when the shelling allowed it.

Dieter worried about his parents. They both seemed to have lost their will to survive. Eva talked continuously under her breath. At first Dieter had tried to listen and respond, asking her to speak up, but she paid no attention. The bits he could hear seemed to be addressed to distant relatives, childhood friends and Reinhard. She even talked to the Rothsteins. Eventually, Dieter gave it up as meaningless rambling.

Most of the time, Ernst sat silently staring at the wall or the people around him. When he spoke, which he did less and less frequently as the siege went on, it was always disturbing. Once he whispered in Dieter's ear, "We have to move close to the entrance."

"I don't think that's a good idea, Father," Dieter had replied. "It's the most dangerous place. What if a shell explodes outside? There is the least protection there."

"Yes, yes," his father had said impatiently, "but when the Russians come, they will use flame throwers on the cellars. Those near the entrance will be killed immediately. That will be better than to linger with horrible burns or, worse, to survive. And the Russians rape all the women — girls, too, younger than ..." Ernst went back to staring at nothing.

Dieter was horrified, but he promised that, when the Russians got close, he would move them to the entrance.

But it was Greta who worried Dieter most. Ever since she had lost her flute, she'd become more and more withdrawn. She would sit for hours, hugging her knees, rocking back and forth and humming to herself. Dieter missed the light, happy sound of her laughter as much as the flute tunes. The world had become a heavier, darker place.

Despite her silence, Greta didn't lose her ability to scrounge. Once, she crawled through the underbrush beside the Landwher Canal for half an hour to steal a fresh fish from the basket of a soldier fishing from the bank. The fish was coarse and bony, but they all ate it with relish.

Another time, Dieter and Greta had come upon a horse killed by a shell. The beast was sitting on its haunches, its glazed eyes staring down the street and its teeth bared in a manic grin. A sloppy pile of greenish entrails lay spilled on the cobbles beside it. A gaggle of women were crudely hacking off pieces of the beast's flanks. Disgusted, Dieter turned away, but Greta rushed forward and began arguing with the women. They tried to push the girl away, but she persisted and eventually was allowed to cut off a piece for herself. She returned to Dieter, silently handed him the bloody hunk of meat and continued the long walk home.

Greta was becoming an animal. As long as she had her sense of humor and took pleasure in her music, Dieter could ignore it, but now there was no looking away. Death held no fear for her, and she showed no disgust at even the most horrible carnage and desolation. Increasingly, she functioned only to secure food and fuel. When Dieter asked her to do something, she responded, but when he tried to talk to her, all he got were grunts and monosyllables. Dieter's entire family were slipping away from him.

+ + +

On April 25, the Americans and the Russians met south of Berlin at Torgau on the River Elbe. That morning, Dieter heard small-arms fire for the first time — and Reinhard came home.

"Dieter! Dieter! Are you in there?"

Dieter heard his brother's voice before he saw him. He stood up. "Over here," he shouted. "Greta, Reinhard's back!"

Greta glanced up from the portable stove, where she was boiling wilted cabbage leaves. Ingrid, who never left her side these days, was tucked securely into her waistband. "Did he bring food?" Greta asked.

"I don't know," Dieter replied, "but he's back. He's alive."

Greta shrugged and returned to her task.

"Hello, Little Brother," Reinhard said.

Never plump, Reinhard was now skeletal. His jaw and cheekbones stood out, and his pale hair seemed thin, adding to his skull-like appearance. His uniform hung off his body, but he managed a bright smile. "Hello, Greta."

Greta looked up. "Hello, Reinhard," she said in a flat voice. "Did you bring food?"

Reinhard hesitated, confused by the odd welcome. "I did," he said eventually.

Immediately, Greta's face brightened. "What?" she asked eagerly.

"Here's something to begin with," Reinhard answered, holding out a can of peaches. Greta grabbed it and rummaged for a can opener.

"I'm glad everyone is all right," Reinhard said uncertainly, looking over at his parents. "Hello, Mother."

Eva ignored Reinhard, continuing an involved conversation with Marcus Rothstein. But Ernst seemed to perk up at his son's arrival. "Reinhard, my boy. I knew you would come back. Now you can put my plan into effect."

"What plan?" Reinhard asked.

"Why, my plan to go to Canada, of course. I've told Dieter all about it and he has Allen's address. But the three of you must leave soon. The sooner you leave, the sooner you can surrender to the Canadians and begin a new life. There's nothing here for young people anymore."

"We're not leaving without you and Mother," Dieter interrupted.

Ernst looked crestfallen.

"Greta," Reinhard said, "divide the peaches between you, Mother and Father. I need to talk with Dieter."

"Okay," Greta said, laying out three bowls.

Dieter felt cheated — peaches were his favorite, and he hadn't had any fruit for so long. But Reinhard beckoned him to the door and up the cellar steps.

Reinhard led the way over the rubble and finally settled down behind a ruined wall. He pulled a sausage out of his pack, broke off a piece and handed it to Dieter. "I rescued this and the peaches from a bombed supply train," he said by way of explanation.

As Dieter ate hungrily, Reinhard asked questions. "What's the matter with everyone?"

Between mouthfuls, Dieter told his brother about the family's odd behavior. Reinhard listened intently. "It's shock," he said, when Dieter had finished. "I've seen it often enough in soldiers, but it happens to civilians, too. Perhaps more so — they are not trained for battle. They need to get out of this place. That's why I wanted to see you alone. There is not much time. The Russians have almost encircled Berlin. The ring will be complete today or tomorrow; then it will be too late."

"What about General Steiner?" Dieter asked, remembering leaflets that had dropped from the air the previous evening. "Hold on!" they had exhorted. "Steiner is coming."

"It's a pipe dream," Reinhard said bitterly. "Steiner has no tanks or ammunition. This is the end. Berlin can't hold out more than a few days. Did you ever get that tattoo?"

"No," Dieter said, confused by the abrupt change of subject. "In all the chaos, they seem to have forgotten that I don't have one."

"Good. Father is right. You must take Greta and head west. The Americans are on the Elbe. You must not let the Russians take you."

"Everyone is telling me where to run to," Dieter said, through a mouthful of sausage. "Mother told me to go to Uncle Walter's farm. Father said I should go to Canada — and now you."

"They're both right," Reinhard said. "Uncle Walter's farm is to the northwest. It would make a good stopping place on the journey. Go there and then carry on until you meet the Canadians."

"I don't think Mother and Father can make it that far," Dieter said.

"You're not listening," Reinhard said urgently. "You and Greta must go. That is the only chance."

"No!" Dieter shouted. "I will not leave Mother and Father. And what about you?"

Reinhard laughed. "Me? My fate was sealed long ago. But you and Greta still have a chance. You must take it."

"No," Dieter repeated.

"Damn it all," Reinhard swore angrily. "Don't you know what we've been doing? Have you been sitting with your head in the sand all these years?"

Dieter looked at his brother blankly.

"Oh hell," Reinhard said resignedly, his eyes drifting away from Dieter as if he were looking into the past.

"In 1943, in the Ukraine — outside some little town I don't even remember the name of," he began softly. "There were nearly two thousand of them — old men, infants, pregnant women, children, rabbis, shopkeepers, writers, carpenters — everyone. The entire Jewish population of the town. They were told they were going to be resettled, that they could bring one suitcase each. They all showed up as ordered in the town square at 7:30 in the morning. Tables were set up so they could register and their names could be checked off against the town records — all very orderly.

"We had five trucks. Each truck held fifty people, so we could take two hundred and fifty at a time. They were driven out of town into a clearing in the woods. They were told to pile their suitcases to one side and to undress. Some were frightened now, or angry, but it was important that they be rushed along because the trucks were on their way back to pick up the next batch, and the first lot had to be processed before they arrived. Those who refused to do as they were told or who did not move quickly enough were beaten or shot by the guards.

"Soon they were ready, old men, young women, children, all naked together. We selected twenty at a time and made them run through the woods to where we had forced some Russian prisoners to dig a deep pit the day before. The Jews were made to line up right at the edge. That way, when they were shot, the bodies would fall neatly into the pit. But some twisted away at the last minute or were still alive when they fell, so a dozen young men were forced into the pits to arrange the bodies in neat rows to save space. At the end of the day, these men became the top layer.

"Some pleaded and begged, some cursed us, some ran into the trees. None escaped. One woman wanted us to take pity on her child. It could have been no more than a year old — a beautiful little girl, blond hair and huge blue eyes. Not at all Jewish looking — she reminded me of Greta as a baby. Anyway, the woman held the child out to us, but no one did anything. Then Alfred shot the woman in the head and threw the child into the pit. We could hear it crying for a long time before one of the men in the pit killed it. Alfred was always the strongest of us.

"It was a long, hard day's work. It was evening before the trucks brought the Russians back to fill in the pit.

"It was special duty, they told us. It had to be done, you know. We must be strong. The Jewish menace must be eradicated. Once we are cleansed, we will win."

Reinhard's voice was flat, as if reciting something he had been forced to learn by heart. "And we believed them, to our eternal damnation. We thought we were strong enough to do this great cleansing. Some were — it never bothered Alfred. But the nightmares ... special duty. It is one thing to kill an enemy in battle, but a child on the edge of a pit ..." Reinhard laughed bitterly.

Dieter sat in horrified silence, staring at his brother as what he was hearing sank in. "All the Jews? All of them?" he asked. "The Rothsteins?"

"The Rothsteins, the Tenenbaums, the Leibowiczes, the Springers. Every Jew in Berlin, and Warsaw, and Prague, and Lodz, and Kiev, and Paris. Millions. A hundred thousand in one ravine outside Kiev. Outside every captured town and village. Some of the men were sent on camp duty and — the stories they came back with!

Places built to kill people with poisoned gas —
Sobibor, Belzec, Treblinka, Auschwitz. Millions.
Up in smoke. Poof. And we did it — the SS. That
was our job — to slaughter an entire people."

Could it be possible? The trains, the camps —
the organization. Could Reinhard have done
this? The brother he had worshiped in his
immaculate new uniform? In his heart, Dieter
knew it made terrible sense.

"Do you understand?" Reinhard asked. "The
Russians know what we have done. They found
the camps, and the graves, and the very few survivors. Do you think they are going to look
kindly on us? Will they make distinctions
between good Germans and bad Germans? No.
We are all damned.

"But the death camps were in the east. The
Americans and the British have not seen the full
horror of it. You must take Greta and go west.
Tell me you will do it."

Dieter was too overwhelmed to answer. Where
was his responsibility? His parents were in phys-
ical danger, but they had been since the bombing
had begun. The Russians would not pay much
attention to an old couple who acted oddly. But
they would certainly pay attention to Greta. She
had just turned twelve, but she was beautiful …
and being a child would be no protection.

But rape wasn't Dieter's only worry about Greta. She would do anything to ensure her survival, including things that Dieter, with all his experience of battle, would hesitate at. Her ruthlessness had served them all well, and she would need it in the hard times coming after the war. But if life became easier, would she go back to normal? Or was this pitiless animal all that remained of her?

Dieter was roused from his thoughts by Greta's voice from behind the ruined wall. "Dieter, Reinhard. Mother and Father are running away!"

"Where are they?"

"They went along the street," Greta replied, running into the open and pointing over the rubble.

Two stumbling figures, the taller supporting the shorter, were making their way slowly through the desolation.

"Mother!" Dieter yelled, as he started after them.

Dieter didn't hear the shell coming. The first thing he knew was a fist punching him in the chest, knocking him backward into Reinhard. Groggily, he staggered to his feet. The street was filled with smoke and dust.

"Father!" he screamed. There was no reply.

Reinhard found them, lying by a wall. Ernst had his arm protectively around Eva. They were unmarked, but both were dead.

Dieter stood numbly before his parents, tears rolling down his cheeks. Then he looked back to see Greta standing a few steps away, calmly regarding the bodies.

Dieter knew then that his parents' actions had been deliberate: Ernst had understood that he and Eva were endangering their children, so he had removed their burden.

"We'll go," Dieter promised.

Reinhard nodded. But Dieter added, "On two conditions. One, we head northwest for the Canadian army and, two, you come with us."

Reinhard thought for a long moment. "Very well," he said at last.

Dieter and Reinhard covered the bodies with rubble as best they could, to keep the dogs away. Then, taking Greta by the hand, they headed down the street through the dust.

Dieter flicked on his flashlight. The beam was almost gone now, but he would not need it much longer. A pale light suffused the eastern sky.

Joe was awake. He looked more alert now as he stared at Dieter. "I saw it," he said. "At Belsen."

"Saw what?" Dieter asked.

"I guess the people outside the wire were the newest arrivals. Most of them were alive. Beyond the wire was a swirling cloud of gray dust — a living thing, heavy with typhus and the smell of death. It was as if God was ashamed of what was inside that wire.

"The dust hid walking skeletons — thousands of them, shuffling among the dead. I guess walking was the only way they could prove they were still alive. Bodies were piled everywhere. From the windows of the huts, faces peered out at us — people too weak to shuffle, who'd been propped against the glass so they could glimpse their liberators before they died."

Joe fell silent, but his gaze never left Dieter's face. "We should have been angry. We should have rushed out of that place and hunted down every one of those monsters with tattoos on their arms and black "Blood and Honor" knives in their pockets."

Dieter couldn't meet Joe's eyes. He knew the Canadian remembered seeing Dieter's own knife. Would he want revenge?

"But we didn't," Joe went on. "The horror was too enormous to understand. How is it possible?"

"I don't know," Dieter replied. He had had nothing to do with the horrors that Reinhard and Joe talked about, yet he felt guilty.

He looked up, nervous, expecting to see disgust or hatred in Joe's eyes. There was neither.

"Go on," Joe said.

"What?" Dieter asked.

"Tell me how you escaped from Berlin." Joe was concentrating hard to keep his eyes on Dieter. Dieter thought he could see the merest hint of a smile. The flashlight flickered and died, leaving Joe's face in deep shadow.

Dieter took a deep breath, "The city was a ruin," he began.

As they walked through Berlin's rubble-strewn streets, Dieter felt only bewildered. Blackened walls stood like decayed cathedrals, their windows open to nothing but the sky. Rooms were ripped apart to expose their most intimate privacy. Curtains flapped forlornly where windows used to be. Chairs waited patiently for owners who would never return. Wardrobes spilled clothing into the street, where ragged shapes, ducking as each shell whined overhead, crawled from cellars to scrounge. A woman wearing a velvet evening gown staggered past clutching the polished marble bust of an ancient Roman emperor.

Dieter chuckled bitterly. "Do you remember the catalog you showed me from the degenerate art exhibition?"

"Yes," Reinhard answered. "What about it?"

"There was a group of pictures in there by artists who called themselves surrealists. I liked those pictures, even though they made me uncomfortable. They showed a world that couldn't exist, where the unexpected was the norm and the rules didn't apply. I suppose Hitler didn't like them because they made you think, and he didn't want anyone to think. It's so ironic."

"What is?" Reinhard asked.

"All this." Dieter made a sweeping gesture at their surroundings. "The war that Hitler created has given us the surreal world he feared so much."

Dieter felt unreasoning laughter welling up inside him. It was so insane it had to be funny. As his laughter escaped, Reinhard looked puzzled, then began laughing, too. Although he didn't understand, it was such a relief to laugh!

Greta walked on in silence.

Their hysteria died in their throats as they turned the next corner. The street was lined with linden trees dressed in new spring foliage. From every tree, a body swung gently in the breeze, each wearing a cardboard placard around its neck announcing its crime: "Deserted his post." "Traitor to the Führer." Greta studied the bodies with detachment.

They were two-thirds of the way along the gruesome line when a familiar voice stopped them. "Hey, Reinhard. You're always missing the fun."

They turned to see Alfred descending the steps of a ruined building. His immaculate black uniform sent a shiver crawling along Dieter's spine. Alfred had his pistol drawn and was herding a frightened middle-aged man in civilian clothes.

"Can you believe it?" Alfred asked. "Just when everyone needs to be strong to face the Reich's greatest trial, there are people disobeying the Führer and trying to escape. We must show ourselves deserving of the Führer's salvation. These scum," Alfred waved vaguely at the hanging bodies, "are not worthy to be National Socialists.

"This one," he said, shoving the cowering man in front of him, "is a sergeant in the Wehrmacht. He should be killing Russians. But where did we find him? Out of uniform, hiding in his pantry. It's disgusting."

"What are you going to do with him?" Reinhard asked.

"Hang him, of course. Like all these other weaklings."

"You can't," Greta said quietly.

Alfred smiled. "Well, little Greta. You are growing into quite the Aryan maiden — you'll soon be ready to breed the new master race. By then, we'll have gotten rid of all deviants, impure stock and cowards. Then the new world will dawn."

"But this man could be useful." Greta was thinking fast. "You have given him a serious scare. He probably realizes his error and is prepared to fight like a demon now. Aren't you?"

The man nodded frantically. "Yes, yes," he said. "I'll kill all the Russians you want."

Alfred looked thoughtful for a moment, then grinned. "All right. Get lost."

A pitifully grateful expression crossed the sergeant's face. "Thank you."

"Go!" Alfred barked impatiently.

The man began a stumbling run down the street. Alfred smiled at Greta, icy, soulless. Then he wheeled, raised his pistol and shot the retreating figure in the back. The man flung his arms to the sides and fell heavily to the ground.

"He would just have run away again." Alfred shrugged. "Now, where are you all going?"

Greta clung tightly to Dieter's waist, but her eyes were hard.

"Our parents were killed by a Russian shell," Reinhard explained calmly. "Dieter and I are taking Greta to the Flak Towers in the Tiergarten. They can withstand anything. She'll be safe there."

"Then you're going back to fight the Russians?" Alfred asked.

"Of course," Reinhard said. "The Führer demands it."

"You know, Reinhard, I have always had doubts about you. You say all the right things, but lately I have felt your heart hasn't been in our task. I suspected an inner flaw would surface when the struggle became difficult. I suppose it was your father — he never accepted National Socialism as he should. It's probably just as well he died."

"Yes," Reinhard agreed, "Ernst was weak."

"Exactly," Alfred smiled. "So, I'll help you. You take the girl to the Flak Towers and I'll take young Dieter to the lines. One more brave soldier for an hour or two might make a difference."

"No," Greta said softly, pushing away from Dieter. "You can't split us up."

"But you were going to be split up anyway. Or were you? By an odd coincidence, the Flak

Towers are in the only direction out of Berlin still not controlled by the Russians. You wouldn't have been running away, would you?"

"Of course not," Reinhard said. "Hell, Alfred, think of what we have been through together. How can you suspect me of running away when the Führer's need is so great?"

Alfred looked uncertain.

"Think about Kursk — we almost died there. And Caen, teaching boys like Dieter to be soldiers. After all that, can you really think I'm running away? How can you suspect —"

Reinhard lunged at Alfred, grabbed the hand that held the pistol and tried to tear it away. With a deafening crash, the pistol fired. Reinhard's body spun to one side, pulling Alfred with him into a jumbled heap in the road. The pistol jerked free and fell with a clatter on the cobbles.

Greta leaped forward and seized the pistol. "Stop!" She pointed the gun at Alfred.

Alfred pulled himself into a sitting position, glaring at Greta. "You had better be prepared to use that, Little Girl," he spat.

"I am." Greta's voice was so cold that Dieter had no doubt she meant it. From the look on Alfred's face, he had no doubt either.

"Dieter," Greta said, "see how Reinhard is."

Reinhard lay propped on one elbow, his face a mask of pain. "Help me sit," he said through gritted teeth as Dieter approached him.

Reinhard's left leg was useless, and a large blood stain was forming on the thigh. A couple of times, he screamed with the pain, but he kept encouraging Dieter until he was sitting, facing Alfred.

"Now," he said to Greta. "Give me … the pistol and … get going. Head west until —"

"We're not leaving you," Greta said firmly.

"Yes you are. The bullet … broke the bone. I'm not going anywhere." Reinhard's face was gray and contorted as waves of pain engulfed him. "But I can keep the pistol on Alfred while you escape."

"If you don't pass out from the pain," Alfred sneered.

"You'd better hope I don't." Reinhard tried to smile. "Because before I do, I will put a bullet in your head. Now give me the gun, Little Sister."

"Let me shoot him," Greta said, with such intensity that a look of terror flitted over Alfred's face.

"That won't help," Reinhard said. "Even if you kill Alfred, your choices are to stay until I bleed to death or to go with Dieter."

For the first time, Greta appeared uncertain; then, slowly, she handed over the pistol. Reinhard's hand was remarkably steady as he pointed the weapon at Alfred's face.

"Come, Greta," Dieter said, taking his sister's hand. "We must go."

Greta still hesitated.

"He's right," Reinhard agreed. "There is not much time. Head west to open country, then go northwest. Find Uncle Walter's farm ... the Canadians or British should be close ... take this."

With great effort, he pushed his pack toward Dieter. "Sausage and bread ... might help. Now, good-bye. Hurry!"

"Good-bye, Reinhard," Dieter said, picking up the pack and pulling Greta's arm.

"Good-bye," Greta said. "I love you." Bending down, she placed her worn and tattered doll on her brother's lap. "Ingrid will keep you company." Reinhard smiled, a warm, open smile that Dieter had not seen since his brother had gone to Russia.

Taking Greta's hand, Dieter stumbled down the street. At the corner, they looked back. The two figures sat immobile in the road, the arm of one held out steadily toward the head of the other.

As they turned the corner, Dieter heard a single shot. They had not gone more than half a block when the second shot echoed between the ruined walls.

Greta was awakened by the roar of the Typhoon flashing at treetop height searching for tanks too slow to find cover. It was almost fully light now.

Joe looked better than he had all night. "I'm thirsty," he said after the plane had gone.

"Me too." Greta sat up and rubbed her eyes. Dieter passed his almost empty bottle. Joe took a sip and passed it to Greta, who tipped it up all the way. "It's finished," she said, handing it back to Dieter.

Joe looked over at Dieter. "You been here all night?" he asked.

Dieter nodded.

"You were telling me stories?"

"Yes."

"I don't remember too much," Joe went on slowly. "Most of the time I just wanted to sleep. I was on the edge of a huge black pit. I wanted to slip over the edge and not ever have to worry about anything again. Your stories kept me up on the edge. I cursed you then, but I reckon I owe you. Not that there's much a wreck like me can offer."

"There is," Dieter said quietly. "We want to go to Canada."

"I seem to remember something about that. To do with the last war, wasn't it?"

"Yes," Dieter said, "and a promise to my father. You told stories, too, last night."

"I did?"

"About the town you grew up in — Berlin."

"It hasn't been called that for a long time." A hint of a smile crossed Joe's bloodstained face.

"I grew up in Berlin here," Dieter went on, "but there is nothing left. And I've got an address — a soldier my father met in his war."

"An address?" Joe asked.

Dieter took the crumpled piece of paper from his pocket. "Zaz-ka-toon," he pronounced uncertainly.

Joe chuckled. "Just don't show up in winter. Look, I'm just a plain soldier. There's not much I can do … but," Joe hurried on, "I owe you for last night. I will do whatever I can. I can make quite a noise when I have to and, hell, a guy who's gone up against a Tiger tank can face down a bunch of bureaucrats. They won't know what hit them."

"Thank you," Dieter said.

"Yes, thank you," Greta added.

"Well, now that that's settled," Joe said, "I guess there's nothing to do but wait for someone to find us. My head feels like it's about to explode. I'm not going anywhere except on a stretcher. Did you finish your story?"

"No," Dieter said.

"Then that's as good a way as any to fill the time. What happened next?"

Dieter hesitated. It had been easy to talk to Joe when he was asleep or delirious. Now that Joe was awake, Dieter felt self-conscious.

"Go on," Joe encouraged. "What am I going to do, broadcast it?"

Dieter took a deep breath. "That afternoon in the streets of Berlin was the most frightening of my life. I think Greta and I were in shock. It was ... well, surreal," he said with a wry smile.

"The zoo in the Tiergarten had been bombed and the trees in the park were full of exotic birds. There were zebras drinking in the ponds and ostriches running among the trees."

"And Rajah," Greta added.

"Yes, Rajah the tiger. He was standing in a clearing, majestic as ever, just looking at all the human insanity around him.

"A stable had been hit, and the horses had panicked as the flames raced through the building. Eventually, a wall collapsed and the horses escaped, but they were on fire — their manes and tails blazing as they ran. Their screams were horrible, much worse than human screams.

"Somehow, walking all night, we made it to the countryside. The roads were packed with terrified people, carrying bags and cases or pushing their belongings in prams and carts. The whole world was heading west.

"I thought the country would be safer than the city, but I was wrong."

The line of black dots on the horizon resolved themselves into four squat, brown planes with large red stars on their wings. One after the other, they flew down the crowded road spraying machine-gun bullets into the mass of panicking refugees. Those who fell were trampled. Dieter grabbed Greta and flung her into the ditch. He lay on top of her until the sound of the planes died away, replaced by a cacophony of groans and cries.

Dieter surveyed the road. Contorted bodies lay everywhere. Many were covered in blood. Most lay still.

"We should leave the road, travel through the fields," Greta suggested as they surveyed the scene. "If we keep the road in sight, we can navigate, but all these people are too tempting a target."

Dieter nodded, and the pair walked in silence, conserving their energy. Since they had left Berlin, Greta seemed to be an automaton, with no interest in her surroundings and no conversation — her occasional comments were strictly practical.

When they came to a small farmhouse, Greta said, "Perhaps they'll have food and water."

Dieter preferred to avoid people, but he was hungry, thirsty and too tired to argue.

As they neared the farmhouse, an unnatural stillness seemed to emanate from it. "Something's wrong," Dieter said.

"What?" Greta asked.

"I don't know. It's too quiet."

"Good. Maybe it's deserted."

The kitchen door stood open. Dieter held back, but Greta slid silently along the wall and slipped in. Dieter had no choice but to follow. In the middle of the room was a large, rough-hewn table set for dinner. Around it sat the family — mother, father, grandmother and three small girls. All had been dead for several days.

Greta rifled through the cupboards.

"Greta! What are you doing?" Dieter exclaimed in horror.

"Looking for food, of course," she replied over her shoulder. "They don't need it."

Even after all they had been through, his sister's callousness frightened him. Covering his nose against the vague, sweet smell that permeated the room, Dieter examined the bodies. They were slumped in their chairs, but otherwise looked almost alive. Their faces were calm and their hands rested on the table or on their laps. All except the mother had closed their eyes in their final moments. She stared blindly over the neat place settings as if watching her dead family eat its meal.

"Poison," Dieter breathed. "They must have taken poison rather than fall into the Russians' hands." He struggled to imagine the courage, or terror, that had driven this family to do such a dreadful thing. Then something caught his eye. The youngest of the daughters was sitting closest to him. She reminded Dieter of Greta before the horror of the war had transformed her. The girl probably hadn't understood what was going to happen, but she had known that it was a special occasion. She was dressed in a fancy frock and her hair was carefully tied in pigtails. On her lap, cradled by one impossibly white arm, lay a gleaming flute.

"Greta," Dieter said, his voice rough with emotion, "come see this."

Her eyes followed Dieter's pointing arm. For an age, she stood gazing at the flute. Then she stepped forward and gently lifted the instrument from the girl's lap. Putting it to her lips, she played a single, perfect note. It seemed to go on forever, traveling around the room, wrapping the family in its purity. As it died away, Greta slumped to the floor and wept.

✦ ✦ ✦

The next afternoon, they crested a low hill and saw a small farm nestled in the valley below.

"If I have navigated correctly," Dieter said, "that should be Uncle Walter's place."

"At last," Greta said, stepping forward. "Let's hurry."

"Get down!" Dieter's voice was barely above a whisper, but there was no mistaking its urgency. Greta obeyed instantly.

On the track down the valley to the farm, a squad of Russian soldiers was working its way along the hedgerow. Farther back, a tank rumbled down the narrow road. With a soldier's eye, Dieter examined the lie of the land.

"Okay," he said. "We'll work our way around the edges of these fields down toward the farm. With luck, we will get there before the Russians see us. If Walter is there, he'll help. If not, perhaps we can hide in the barn."

"All right." Greta's voice was a monotone. Throughout the day, she had spoken only to agree with whatever her brother suggested. She was exhausted, and Dieter was worried that she couldn't go much farther. But he was more worried about what might happen to her if the Russians caught them.

"Come on," he encouraged, "it's not far. We can make it."

Keeping to hedges and ditches, the pair worked their way toward the farm. By the time they reached the edge of the farmyard, the Russians were still some distance away.

"Thank heavens they are being cautious," Dieter whispered.

The farm was run down and weeds grew here and there in the yard, but the vegetable plot was carefully tended. On their left, a few scrawny chickens scrabbled in the dirt underneath a raised coop that stood alongside a row of empty pig pens. On their right sat the small farmhouse with the curtains pulled and the door closed. In front of them stood the barn, its door open invitingly.

Dieter led the way across the yard, darting from one patch of cover to the next. He was halfway across the final stretch, with Greta at his heels, when the man with the shotgun stepped out of the barn's darkness. Dieter skidded to a halt.

The man wore dirty, patched work clothes, and he was older than Ernst, but the shotgun was held perfectly steady as it pointed at Dieter's stomach.

"What do you want here?"

Was this Uncle Walter? Dieter didn't remember ever meeting him. He felt very conscious of his tattered SS uniform, but he hadn't had a chance to get rid of it. He had removed the insignia, but it was obviously still a military uniform.

"We're looking for Walter Schell. My name's Dieter Hammer. This is Greta. Our mother was Eva Schell. She was killed in Berlin. So was our father, Ernst. We're trying to get to Canada. The Russians are coming."

The old man looked at them sternly. Dieter's heart was pounding. Any minute he expected Russian soldiers to appear around the corner of the farmhouse.

"I know the Russians are coming," the man said. "It is the best thing that has ever happened to Germany, although Ernst would probably disagree with me." He lowered the shotgun. "I *am* Walter."

A wave of relief swept over Dieter. His knees felt weak. The rumble of the Russian tank sounded very close.

"We have some catching up to do," Walter said, stepping forward, "but first we should get you out of that uniform. Undress and I will get something for you to wear." He moved across the yard to the farmhouse.

Dieter began stripping off his jacket. A movement in the blackness of the barn caught his eye. He stopped and squinted into the gloom, then a figure stepped forward into the sunlight. Dieter gasped. He was much thinner than when Dieter had last seen him, but his big nose and studious glasses made him instantly recognizable.

"Marcus!" Dieter exclaimed.

"Hello, Dieter," Marcus said in his soft voice.

The Jewish boy and the SS soldier stood staring at each other as if transfixed.

"Oh, Marcus," Greta blurted, "I thought you were dead. Your parents were resettled ..." Her voice trailed off.

"I suspected," Marcus said.

"What are you doing here?" Dieter asked.

"Hiding. Helping with the heavy work when it has been safe. Surviving. More than three years now."

"I see you two have met." Walter had returned with an old suit and threadbare sweater. "Put this on," he said, handing it to Dieter. It was much too big, but Dieter didn't care.

Marcus took the discarded SS uniform and Dieter's pack into the barn to hide.

Dieter had just buttoned the trousers when Marcus returned from the barn — and the soldier appeared round the side of the house. He was wearing a helmet and a loose-fitting light brown uniform, and was swinging a small machine gun wildly at the four people in the farmyard. They hurriedly raised their hands in surrender.

The soldier shouted something unintelligible and was joined by three companions. They seemed uncertain what to do. Eventually, one of them stepped forward and pointed his gun at Dieter. "Fascist?" he asked in heavily accented German. Dieter shook his head emphatically.

The soldier repeated the question to each of the others and received the same reply. The process appeared to exhaust the man's German vocabulary, and he lapsed into silence while his companions spread out around the yard. Suddenly, one of the chickens squawked and sprinted into the open. The effect was electrifying. With their hands still in the air, Dieter, Greta, Marcus and Walter watched as the four soldiers, yelling frantically, tore around the yard after the chicken. The uproar disturbed the other chickens, which flew from under the coop. Soon the farmyard was a mass of running, shouting men and hysterical chickens.

The soldiers were so engrossed in the chase that they failed to notice the tank's arrival. In a cloud of dust, it ground noisily to a halt at the farmyard gate, its cannon pointing threateningly into the yard.

With a heavy clank, the hatch on the tank's turret swung open and an officer emerged. He jumped to the ground and fired his pistol in the air. Immediately, the soldiers stopped, two with dead chickens in their grasp.

The officer barked a series of orders in angry Russian and the soldiers leaped into action, dropping their booty. One man went into the barn, another into the house and the last two toward the coop and sties. The officer walked over to the prisoners and examined each in turn. He stared particularly long and hard at Dieter. "Who are you?" he asked in reasonable German.

Dieter was frantically searching for a plausible reply when the soldier from the barn burst back into the yard, shouting in Russian. In front of him, he clutched Dieter's SS shirt. He handed the shirt to the officer, who examined it carefully, then raised his hand and rested the muzzle of his pistol against Dieter's forehead. Dieter felt sweat form beneath the dirt on his skin.

"That is yours?" the officer asked. "You are a Fascist."

Dieter wasn't sure whether the latter was a statement or a question. Either way, he didn't like it. "No," he said weakly. The officer cocked his pistol with a deafening click. The sweat began to run down Dieter's skin.

"Please don't shoot him." Marcus's calm voice came from Dieter's left. The officer turned his head, but the pistol remained, cold and hard, against Dieter's forehead.

"Why not?" the officer asked.

"He is not a Nazi," Marcus explained. "It is not his uniform. A soldier came yesterday and stole some clothes. He must have left his uniform in the barn. Dieter is the farmer's son. They are good people. They have hidden me from the Fascists. I am a Jew."

The officer chewed his lip as he gazed thoughtfully at Marcus. "Say a Jewish prayer," he said. Marcus recited something in a language Dieter had never heard.

The officer lowered his pistol. "Take off your jacket and sweater," he ordered. Dieter obeyed. The officer grabbed Dieter's left wrist and twisted it painfully as he examined the inside of Dieter's upper arm. Satisfied, he let it go.

A wave of relief swept over Dieter — it was all he could do to keep his legs from buckling beneath him. The officer turned and shouted orders to his men. Picking up the dead chickens, they trotted out of the yard and down the road.

The officer climbed back into his tank and, with a loud crunching of gears, it reversed and followed the men. Silence fell on the yard. Dieter realized that they all still had their hands in the air. He lowered his and put his sweater and jacket back on.

"Thank you," he said, turning to Marcus.

Marcus shrugged. "There has been enough killing. Just be glad I could remember the Friday night Kiddish. But it might not work next time."

"I know," Dieter said. "We'll go."

"Oh no," Greta groaned. "I can't. Not another step." She collapsed into a disconsolate heap in the dirt.

"We must," Dieter said.

"Why can't we stay here?"

"Because the Russians will come back. Besides, we have to get to Canada."

"I don't want to go to Canada," Greta wailed. "I want to stay here."

Dieter looked around helplessly.

"Your brother is right," Walter said gently. "It would not be wise to stay here. But rest and have something to eat. There is still some bacon from the last pig. I'll find it." Walter walked to the house.

Dieter turned to Marcus and asked the one question that had been swirling around his head. "How did you end up here?"

"Your mother," he said.

"Mother?"

"Yes." Marcus went on with a smile, "When things got bad for us in Berlin, your mother talked to my mother and arranged for me to come here. Walter couldn't hide us all, but he could take me, and I could work. Let me show you my house."

Dieter and Greta followed Marcus to the cool barn. On the way, they had a long drink from the rain barrel — fresh, clean water, not like the warm metallic-tasting stuff from Dieter's water bottle.

Marcus led them to the rear of the barn. With a rake, he scratched away some hay and loose earth to reveal a trapdoor in the wooden floor. Hauling it open, he indicated the dark hole below.

"My home of the last three years," he said. "I'm afraid I can't invite you in, but you are welcome to have a look."

Dieter and Greta stepped forward and peered over the edge. Beneath the trapdoor was a square room, barely wide enough for Marcus to lie down in, and slightly less deep. The floor was rough wooden planks — the walls damp, crumbling earth. Some blankets made a rough bed against one wall; beside it stood a low table with a notebook, a pen and a half-burned candle.

"Damp and cold in winter, but safe."

"It's horrible," Greta said.

Marcus laughed. "Yes," he agreed, "it is fairly grim, but much better than many had, I think."

"Why couldn't you live in the house?" she insisted.

"That would have been far too dangerous — neighbors were always dropping in, and not all of them were as ... sympathetic as Walter. He ran a great risk in hiding me. If I'd been discovered, he would have been shot. I am not sure you know what an exceptional relation you have in Walter.

"We didn't have it too bad. We ate reasonably well — although I do not think my parents would be happy about all the pork. My parents ... Tell me what happened to them? In the first months, I received the occasional message from Mother, but they stopped more than two years ago."

Dieter shuddered at the image of the Rothsteins, naked on the edge of some hellish pit. He took a deep breath to calm himself. "They were taken away in the big roundup of February twenty-seventh, nineteen forty-three," he said. "I saw them both being loaded into a truck. I never saw them after that."

"But you know ... you suspect what happened?"

"The newspapers said they were being resettled in the east."

"But that was a lie. Tell me what you know," Marcus pleaded.

"Greta," Dieter said, "could you fill the water bottle at the rain barrel outside?"

Greta nodded and left.

"I truly don't know what happened," Dieter said quietly, "but Reinhard told me that resettlement was a lie. All the people on the trains east were sent to special camps to be ... Perhaps ..." Dieter's voice trailed off.

"I didn't —" Dieter began, but Marcus interrupted him.

"No, there are no words for this. Go find your Canadians."

"What will you do?"

Marcus shrugged. "Go back to Berlin when the fighting is over. I have to be certain. Then, who knows? Perhaps Palestine. I don't want to run away from Berlin — it's my home and to leave would mean that Hitler had won. But I don't know if I could live there. I think there will be too many ghosts. Perhaps we both need to leave."

They were interrupted by Greta's return and by Walter's shout that a meal was ready. They ate rapidly — everyone nervous about the Russians returning. Dieter told Walter what had happened in Berlin. When they had finished eating, Dieter retrieved his pack from the barn. Walter gave them some bread for the road and told them what he knew about where the British and Canadians might be. In a flurry of hand-shakes, thanks and good wishes, Dieter and Greta set off again.

Dieter was sorry to leave. All hope had been centered on a new life in Canada, but Walter's existence and Marcus's survival suggested that a future, however hard, could be had in Germany.

At the top of the hill, Dieter paused to look back on the tiny farm, looking so peaceful below. Then he turned and headed northwest. Two days later, the pair came upon a burning Tiger tank.

"That's quite the tale," Joe said, looking hard at Dieter. "I reckon Canada's going to seem pretty boring after all you've been through."

"I think we will like boring," Dieter said.

Joe's eyes drifted over to Greta. "Can you play that thing?" he asked, indicating the flute tucked into the waistband of her dress.

"Of course," she replied indignantly.

"Well, give us a tune. It might help the boys find us."

Greta began to play. High, glasslike notes drifted onto the morning air.

It was full daylight when the last notes of Greta's song floated away and the patrol found them — three soldiers from Joe's anti-tank unit. One kept a wary eye on Dieter and Greta while a second attended to Joe's wound and the third checked the wrecked tank.

"They'll give you a medal for this," said the one bandaging Joe. "Those Tigers ain't easy to stop."

"Yeah," Joe agreed. "I can use it as a plate for this hole in my skull."

The soldier laughed. "So where'd you find these two?" he asked.

"They showed up last night."

"Nazis?" the soldier asked.

"Nah," Joe said, looking over at Dieter, "just kids trying to escape. They want to go to Saskatoon."

"Funny. They look like smart kids." The soldier chuckled. "What are we going to do with them?"

"Take them back with us. They'll have to go to one of those refugee camps. I promised I would help them, so I'll do what I can. This wound'll keep me around for a while, so I'll keep track of them."

The first soldier tied off the bandage and sat back to admire his handiwork. "That should stop whatever brains you have left from falling out."

"I can afford to lose a few before I get to your level."

"You sure did a number on that Tiger." The third soldier scrambled down into the ditch. "I reckon it was already damaged and the rocket went in an open hatch. That's the only way it could brew up so fast. Rockets usually just bounce off those things."

"There was nothing wrong with its gun," Joe replied. "Ask Tom about that."

The three soldiers glanced instinctively at their comrade's body. "We'll send a burial party back for him," the first said. "Bad luck, right at the end.

"Hey, Joe, you won't have heard. It was on German radio last night — Hitler's dead. They said he died fighting the Russians in the ruins of Berlin. The Russians say he committed suicide. Who cares? Berlin's done for, too. The Russians raised a flag on the Reichstag yesterday. Reckon that about ends it."

Dieter had understood very little of the soldiers' conversation and looked questioningly at Joe.

"Hitler's dead," Joe translated. "Berlin's fallen. The war's over."

"Good!" Greta said firmly.

Dieter agreed, but he felt confusion as well. Hitler had been a part of his life as long as he could remember, and the war had been on since he was a kid. Now he was seventeen and life would be odd without either.

Canada was going to be very strange, but at least there would be fewer ghosts. Dieter put his arm around Greta. His sister returned his hug.

"I think we'll be all right," he said, trying to convince himself.

"Of course," Greta replied. "We have to be."

AUTHOR'S NOTE

The historical background of Dieter's story is accurate. For example, Luz Long was the first to congratulate Jesse Owens at the Berlin Olympics, a Berlin ration line was destroyed by Russian shelling on April 21, 1945, and flaming horses did run in terror through the Tiergarten. Many scenes are based on documented events. Joe's description of Belsen is taken from a radio broadcast given by Richard Dimbleby, one of the first Western reporters to see the horrors of the Holocaust. Minor points of chronology and place have been altered in the interest of a coherent story, but I trust not so much that purists will be offended.

In telling this story from the perspective of a German boy who joins the SS, it is not my intention to apologize for the Nazis. They, and particularly the SS, richly deserve the abhorrence that the civilized world feels for the values they held and the atrocities they committed. What I have tried to do is imagine what it was like for those who came of age in the nineteen-thirties and -forties, indoctrinated from earliest days and swept up in circumstances they could never understand. To have been a teenager in Nazi Germany must have been immensely difficult, and to expect one to have had a rational post-war perspective is unreasonable. The lure of uniforms and flags and the flood of propaganda must have been next to irresistible. Dieter is probably exceptional in questioning as much as he does.

Flames of the Tiger is an adventure story. If there is an underlying message, it is this: Always question what people tell you is a self-evident truth, especially when everyone tells you the same thing.

ACKNOWLEDGMENTS

There are many excellent books on the Second World War. For my purposes, Leonard Gross's *The Last Jews in Berlin* and Cornelius Ryan's *The Last Battle* were particularly helpful in giving insight into what life must have been like for Berliners in the spring of 1945.

I found many Web sites with much useful, otherwise difficult-to-obtain, detail on uniforms, regiments, the SS, etc. However, if you decide to do a Web search on your own, beware — there are some strange people out there, who keep alive Hitler's vision.

Again my thanks go to Charis Wahl for encouraging me to make this story as good as it could be.